"Your village is delightful."

James sat back in his seat, driving slowly through the narrow streets.

"Well, I like it, but I was born here," Matilda replied, then went on to ask, "Have you known Dr. Bramley long?"

"Er—he and my father knew each other in their youth."

"Oh, well, I didn't think you were all that old," said Matilda kindly. "Dr. Bramley must be getting on."

Her companion allowed himself a faint smile. "I am thirty-eight," he told her. "And how old are you, Miss ffinch?"

"Me? Oh, twenty-six."

"And heart-whole?"

A difficult question to answer. "Well, I was.... Are you married?"

"No, but I'm engaged."

Matilda knew exactly how a pricked balloon must feel....

Betty Neels is well-known for her romances set in the Netherlands, which is hardly surprising. She married a Dutchman and spent the first twelve years of their marriage living in Holland and working as a nurse. Today, she and her husband make their home in an ancient stone cottage in England's West Country, but they return to Holland often. She loves to explore tiny villages and tour privately owned homes there, in order to lend an air of authenticity to the background of her books.

Books by Betty Neels

THE MOST MARVELLOUS SUMMER

Betty Neels

Harlequin Books

TORONTO • NEW YORK • LONDON
AMSTERDAM • PARIS • SYDNEY • HAMBURG
STOCKHOLM • ATHENS • TOKYO • MILAN

Original hardcover edition published in 1991
by Mills & Boon Limited

ISBN 0-373-03185-8

Harlequin Romance first edition March 1992

THE MOST MARVELLOUS SUMMER

CHAPTER ONE

MATILDA had fallen in love. She had had no intention of doing so, but there it was. She first saw the stranger during the reading of the first lesson by Sir Benjamin Fox, whose pompous voice, pronouncing biblical names with precise correctness, always set her thoughts wandering. She glanced along the pew at her two brothers, home for the half-term holidays, her two sisters and her mother and then allowed her gaze to wander to the manor pew at the side of the chancel, where Lady Fox sat with various members of her family. They all looked alike, she thought, with their fine beaky noses and thin mouths. She turned her head very slightly and looked across the main aisle and saw the stranger sitting by Dr Bramley. He appeared a very large man with broad shoulders, fair hair which she suspected had a sprinkling of grey, and a splendid profile. A pity that he didn't look round... Sir Benjamin rolled the last unpronounceable name off his tongue and she fixed her eyes on him once more—green eyes, shadowed by sweeping black lashes, in a lovely face crowned by a wealth of copper hair.

Her father announced the hymn and the congregation rose to sing it cheerfully, galloping ahead of the organ when it had the chance, and then sitting once more for the second lesson. The headmaster of the village infants' school read it in a clear unhurried voice and this time she listened, until something compelled her to glance across the aisle again. The stranger was looking at her and he was every bit as handsome as she had expected him to be; unsmiling—it wouldn't have done in church if he had smiled anyway—and somehow compelling. She went faintly pink and looked away from him quickly, feeling all at once as though she were in some kind of blissful heaven, knowing with certainty that she had fallen in love. It was a delightful sensation, and she pondered over it during her father's sermon, taking care not to look across the aisle again; the village was a small one and rather isolated, so that everyone was inclined to mind everyone else's business and turn a molehill into a mountain, preferably a romantic one, and that if a girl so much as glanced twice at the same man. She was aware that the village was disappointed that she hadn't married. She had had three proposals and although she had hesitated over them she had declined them kindly and watched her erstwhile suitors marry without regret. Twenty-six was getting on a bit, as Mrs Chump at the general stores so often reminded her, but she had waited. Now here he was, the man she wished to marry, dropped as it were from heaven into her path. He could of course be married, engaged or a confirmed bachelor—she would have to find out, but, as she was great friends with Dr Bramley, it would be easy to ask him.

The last hymn sung, the congregation filed out, stopping to chat as it went, and since the rector's family were well liked their progress was slow; they arrived at the church door just in time for her to see the stranger, still with the doctor, talking to Sir Benjamin, and even as Matilda looked Lady Fox tapped him on an arm and pushed Roseanne, her eldest daughter, forwards. Matilda watched him being swept away down the tree-lined avenue which led to the manor-house from the churchyard.

She watched him go, already planning to ask who he was when she got to the manor-house in the morning. Esme, her younger sister, fourteen and as sharp as a needle, tugged her arm. 'Hey, Tilly—come on,' and then, 'I bet you've fallen for him—I have. A bit old for me I suppose, but he'd do nicely for you.'

'Rubbish, love. What nonsense you do talk.'

'You went all pink when he looked at you—I expect it was your hair—it kind of glows, you know, even under a hat!'

They started to walk along the narrow path which led to the rectory garden and Esme said, 'Hilary's seen him too, but of course she's engaged...'

'Let's forget him,' said Matilda cheerfully. 'We'll probably never see him again.' She uttered the remark with the heartfelt wish that it might not be true. However could she marry anyone else now that she had seen him and knew that she had fallen in love at last? She would have to stay an old maid, if there was such a thing these days, helping with the parish and wearing dreary hats and worthy undateable clothes.

She sighed heavily at the very idea and Esme said, 'I bet you'll meet again—I dare say he's your fate.'

'Oh, what romantic nonsense,' said Matilda again and hurried to the kitchen to help her mother dish up the Sunday lunch.

Her mother had her head in the Aga oven, and was prodding the joint with a fork. 'Put the apples on for the sauce, will you, dear? I wonder who that giant was in church? Did you see him?' She didn't wait for an answer. 'He seemed to know the Foxes. I must keep my ears open in the village tomorrow.'

She emerged and closed the oven door, an older version of her lovely daughter although the hair was streaked with grey. 'That was a frightful hat Lady Fox was wearing—I wonder where she buys them?'

'Probably makes them herself.' Matilda was peeling apples and biting at the cores.

She was up early the next morning and while her mother cooked the breakfast she sorted the wash, got the machine going, made sure that Esme was up and had everything she needed before catching the bus to Sherborne where she was having extra coaching for her O Levels, and then roused the two boys. Hilary, her other sister, was going to stay with her fiancé and was already up, doing the last of her packing. They all sat down to breakfast presently, a meal taken with the minimum of conversation since everyone there had his or her plans for the day. Esme was the first to go, then the boys on a fishing expedition, the rector to visit a parishioner in hospital at Salisbury and then Hilary, leaving Mrs ffinch and Matilda to clear the table and leave the dishes for Mrs Coffin, who came three times a week to help in the house.

'Don't be late,' warned Mrs ffinch as Matilda got Nelson the cat's breakfast. She sighed as she said it— it irked her that her beautiful daughter should have to go to work each day. Not that it wasn't a suitable job for the daughter of the rector—social secretary to Lady Fox—even though it was badly paid and covered a multitude of odd jobs which no social secretary cognisant with her normal duties would have coun- tenanced. But, as Matilda pointed out, it paid for her clothes, and the fees for Esme's coaching, and helped towards the upkeep of the rectory, a large, rambling house with out-of-date plumbing always going wrong, draughty rooms and a boiler which swallowed coke by the ton. All the same, it was comfortable in a shabby way and the family was a happy one.

It was only a few minutes' walk to the manor-house; Matilda nipped smartly through the light rain and went in through the side-door—not that she wasn't expected to use the front entrance, but the polished floor of the wide hall showed every mark from damp feet and she was aware that Mrs Fletcher from the village, who obliged each day at the manor-house, would have just finished polishing it. She went along the passage to the kitchen, wished Cook and the kitchen maid good morning and made her way through the baize door into the front of the house. Lady Fox was coming down the staircase, holding a handful of letters.

'Good morning, Matilda.' She glanced at the long case clock in the hall, but since Matilda was exactly on time and she had no cause to find fault she went on, 'Such a number of letters this morning; really, my days are so busy...'

Lady Fox gave Matilda a faintly disapproving look; there was nothing wrong with her appearance—the striped shirt, navy pleated skirt and sensible shoes were, to say the least, not worthy of a second glance— but dowdy clothes couldn't dim the brightness of Matilda's hair or the sparkling green of her eyes, and those allied to a delightful nose, a curving mouth and a complexion as smooth and fresh as a child's. Lady Fox frowned slightly, remembering Roseanne's regrettable spots and unfortunate nose. 'I have guests for lunch,' she observed. 'I had better see Cook at once while you deal with these.' She handed the letters to Matilda and hurried away kitchenwards.

Matilda, sorting out butcher's and grocer's bills from invitations to dinner and requests from charities, reflected that Lady Fox wasn't in a very good mood and, since there was no sign of that lady, she put the letters on the desk in Lady Fox's sitting-room and went along to the chilly little room where she arranged the flowers. The gardener had brought in early tulips and daffodils and some rather overpowering greenery and she was trying to decide what to do with them when Lady Fox's voice, high and penetrating, reached her. 'You might do a small centre-piece for the table, Matilda—go into the garden and see what you can find.'

Matilda, well brought up as she had been, allowed herself the comfort of a childish grimace; if it hadn't been for the useful money needed at the rectory, she would have liked to flounce out of the manor-house and never go back.

The garden was soothing, if chilly, and she took a basket with her and picked primulas and grape-hyacinths, late Christmas roses, lily of the valley and a handful of brightly coloured polyanthus and bore the lot back through the garden door and into the hall, intent on fetching a particular bowl which would look just right on the dining-room table.

Lady Fox was in the hall, talking animatedly to the stranger. She paused to look at Matilda and her companion looked too; Matilda, her fiery head a little untidy, her pretty face glowing from the fresh air, clutching her basket of flowers, was worth looking at.

'There you are,' observed Lady Fox with distinctly false *bonhomie*, 'but shouldn't you be arranging the

flowers?' She turned to the man beside her. 'My com-
panion-secretary, you know—I couldn't manage
without help and Roseanne has her painting—quite
talented.'

He gave her a grave, enquiring look and she went
on hurriedly, 'This is Matilda ffinch, the rector's eldest
daughter—Matilda, this is Mr Scott-Thurlow.'

Matilda transferred the basket to her other arm and
held out a hand, to have it engulfed by his large firm
grasp. Now that she could look at him face to face,
she was even more certain that this was the man she
had been waiting for. She beamed at him, full of
delight, and he smiled a little in return. A firm mouth,
perhaps a rather stern one, and his eyes were blue,
heavy-lidded and cool; he would be at least thirty-
five, perhaps nearer forty.

His polite 'How do you do?' was uttered in a deep
quiet voice and her smile widened. Her 'hello' sounded
like that of a little girl who had just been offered
something she had longed for.

Lady Fox spoke in the voice she kept for recalci-
trant children on those occasions when she had been
asked to give away the Sunday school prizes.

'If you would see to the flowers, Matilda—and since
I shan't need you for a few hours you may go home
for your lunch.'

'Back after lunch?' asked Matilda.

'Half-past two.' Mr Scott-Thurlow would be gone
by then; Roseanne on her own could be quite
charming, reflected her fond parent, and there would
be no competition...

'Very well, Lady Fox.' Matilda turned an emerald
gaze upon Mr Scott-Thurlow. Her goodbye was
cheerful; having found him she didn't for one moment

expect fate to lose him again for her. She would have liked to have stayed for lunch—usually she did—but one lunch more or less would make no difference to the future.

She nipped smartly to the back of the house, arranged the flowers and then took herself off home. She passed Roseanne as she left the house, and since she was a kind-hearted girl she was sorry to see that she was wearing an expensive two-piece in the wrong shade of green—it showed up the spots.

Roseanne stopped when she saw her. 'I hate this outfit,' she declared, quite fiercely for her. 'Mother says it's elegant but I feel a fool in it.' She cast an envious eye upon Matilda's person. 'You always look right—why?'

'I don't know. You'd look nice in the greeny blue...'

'There's that man coming to lunch,' went on Roseanne unhappily. 'Mother says I must exert myself...'

She hurried indoors and Matilda went back to the rectory to give her mother and father a hand, prepare the lunch and then sit down and eat it.

'You aren't usually home at this time,' remarked her father, ladling shepherd's pie into exact portions.

'Got the sack?' asked Guy, and Thomas added, 'Shouldn't be surprised with that hair.'

'Visitors for lunch,' explained Matilda, ignoring her brothers. 'I'm to go back at half-past two.'

'You usually stay there even when there are visitors,' mused her mother.

Matilda turned limpid eyes upon her parent. 'Probably I'd have made the numbers wrong, Mother.' She handed out the plates. 'Is it Esme's evening for dancing class? Do you want me to collect her?'

'Well, that would be nice, dear; the bus takes so long to get here.'

Matilda went back to the manor-house after lunch and found Lady Fox and Roseanne arguing about the green outfit. They both looked cross and Lady Fox said at once, 'This silly girl has been invited to stay in London and she doesn't want to go...'

Matilda had collected the second post as she went in, and she sat down and began to sort it. 'Why not?' she asked, pleasantly. 'I should think it would be the greatest fun.'

'I don't know anyone,' mumbled Roseanne.

'Well, you don't expect to until you're there,' said Matilda reasonably, 'but think of the theatres—you know, *The Phantom of the Opera* and *Aspects of Love* and *Cats* and there'll be exhibitions at the Tate and the National Gallery. You might meet some artists.'

Roseanne brightened. 'Well, yes—I suppose that I might; perhaps it wouldn't be so bad.'

Matilda went home again after tea, taken off a tray while she added up the household accounts for Lady Fox. It was a fine evening and the drive to Sherborne would be pleasant. Abner Magna was only a few miles from that town, but the roads were narrow and winding and the evening bus which Esme sometimes took stopped whenever someone wanted to board it or get off, making the journey twice as long. Matilda got a thick knitted jacket, poked at her hair and went to tell her mother that she was about to leave. There was no one in the kitchen but there were voices in her father's study. She opened the door, stuck her head round it and cried, 'I'm off to fetch Esme, we shouldn't be——' She came to a halt; Mr Scott-

Thurlow was standing beside her father, surveying the rather untidy garden.

He said at once, 'Good evening, Miss ffinch,' and her father said mildly, 'John Bramley asked Mr Scott-Thurlow to bring a book over which he had promised to lend me. You have met?'

'Very briefly,' observed his guest. 'I mustn't keep you, sir. Do I understand Miss ffinch to say that she is driving into Sherborne? I'm on the point of going there myself and shall be glad to offer her a lift.'

A delightful prospect, which she had to refuse with regret. 'I'm going to fetch my sister—she's at dancing class, and we've no way of getting back here—the last bus would have gone ...'

'I shall be coming back; I have to take something to the hospital for Dr Bramley, a matter of five minutes. We could collect your sister and I can stop at the hospital on our way back.'

'Oh, well, yes—thank you very much. Do you want to go now?'

'Certainly.' He said all the right things to the rector and then stopped in the hall for a moment to bid Mrs ffinch goodbye before ushering Matilda outside.

He opened the door of the car standing there and she skipped inside. 'What a treat,' she declared happily, 'a Rolls-Royce—wait till Esme sees it.' She added the information that such a vehicle was seldom seen in Abner Magna. 'Of course Sir Benjamin has a Daimler, but it's a bit worthy if you know what I mean.'

He made some non-committal answer, but since she felt strangely at ease with him she enlivened their short journey with odds and ends of information, all of them good-natured, about the village and its inhabitants. 'I dare say you live in London?' she wanted to know.

Mr Scott-Thurlow was sitting back, not driving fast; he said idly, 'Yes, I do. Your village is delightful.'

'Well, I like it, but I was born here. Have you known Dr Bramley long?'

'Er—he and my father knew each other in their youth...'

'Oh, well, I didn't think you were all that old,' said Matilda kindly. 'Dr Bramley is always saying that he'll retire so he must be getting on a bit.'

Her companion allowed himself a faint smile. 'I am thirty-eight,' he told her. 'And how old are you, Miss ffinch?'

'Me? Oh, twenty-six.'

'And heart-whole?'

A difficult question to answer. 'Well, I was... Are you married?'

They were in Sherborne now and he asked, 'Which way?' before saying, 'No, but I'm engaged.'

Matilda knew exactly how a balloon must feel when it was pricked. She said in a rigid voice, 'I expect you're looking forward to getting married. Here we are.'

He stopped the car and turned to look at her. 'Do you know, Miss ffinch, I cannot remember when I was cross-examined so thoroughly?'

She stared at him, stricken. 'I'm sorry, I didn't mean to pry—I just wanted—I was interested...'

He smiled then and her heart turned over. 'I rather enjoyed it. Is that your sister waving to us from the other side of the road?'

A snub, a gentle one, but still a snub. Matilda went a delightful pink and frowned ferociously, remembering the string of questions she had flung at him; he probably thought her a dull country woman with nothing better to do than poke her nose into other people's affairs. Her daydream had been shattered by a few well-chosen words on his part and life would never be the same again. The quicker he went away and she never set eyes on him again the better. She said in a sober voice, 'Yes, that's Esme.'

It was a good thing that Esme elected to sit beside him and chatter non-stop so that Matilda had no need to say much; she thanked him rather primly as he stopped at the rectory gates but it was Esme who urged him to go in with them. An invitation he declined pleasantly enough.

He had gone the next day, or so it seemed from a remark her father made the following evening, and it was then that she realised that she had no idea what he did or who he really was. He had the calm self-assured manner of a solicitor and she had heard him discussing a point of law with the rector during his brief visit. Solicitors, she had always supposed, earned themselves a good living, good enough to run a Rolls—she allowed her thoughts to wander—he might have to get a cheaper car when he married though; his wife would want clothes and the children would need to be educated. She made a resolution then and there not to think about him any more. That she had fallen in love with a man who was on the point of getting married to some other girl was a trick of unkind fate, and there was nothing to do about it.

A week went by, the boys went back to school and so did Esme, and Hilary was home again. Matilda's days were full: Lady Fox each day, choir practice on Thursday evening, Sunday school, driving her father

to one or two of the more distant farms; the pattern
of her future, reflected Matilda, indulging in a rare
attack of self-pity, and then forgetting to be sorry for
herself when she went for a Sunday afternoon stroll
through the woods above the village. It really was a
delightful day; the sky was blue, the trees were turning
green even as she looked at them and there were lambs
racing around the fields, and when she sat on a tree
stump to get her breath a squirrel came and sat within
a yard or two of her. There were compensations, she
told herself stoutly.

She was surprised to find Lady Fox waiting for her
in the hall when she went there on the Monday
morning. She wondered uneasily if she had done
something really dire, like sending a letter in the wrong
envelope, but from the smile on Lady Fox's face she
thought that unlikely.

'There you are, Matilda,' said Lady Fox unnecessarily. 'Come into the sitting-room, will you? I should
like a word with you.'

She nodded to a chair and Matilda sat down, wondering what to expect.

'Roseanne,' began Lady Fox, 'has consented to pay
a visit to London—her godmother, you know, the
Honourable Mrs Venables. I am delighted; she is
bound to meet people.' Lady Fox really meant young
men free to marry. 'There is simply no one of her age
and class here.'

Matilda said nothing, although that was difficult;
the ffinches had been in and around Dorset for cen-
turies and were as good, if not better than the Foxes,
and what was more her mother was distantly related
to a peer of the realm—so distant, it must be said,

that her family name was a mere dot on the outskirts of the lordly family tree—all the same, it was there.

'Such a pity,' went on Lady Fox in what she considered to be a confidential voice, 'that Mr Scott-Thurlow is engaged to be married, although of course he would have been rather old for Roseanne—a pity that I wasn't told.'

'You were telling me about Roseanne's visit,' prompted Matilda while she thought about Mr Scott-Thurlow.

'I am coming to that. She will go only on the condition that you go with her. The visit is for a month and you would go as her companion. Her godmother has no objection, and I shall of course pay you your usual salary. In a week's time.'

'I'll talk it over with my mother and father,' said Matilda in a quiet voice which her nearest and dearest would have recognised as the first sign of rage coming to the boil. 'I shall want to consider it myself.'

Lady Fox looked astounded. 'But my dear girl, it is such a splendid opportunity for you to see something of the sophisticated world—you might even meet some suitable young man. If you are worried about clothes I'm sure——'

'No, I'm not worried about clothes, Lady Fox. I'm not sure that I want to go to London. I really must have a day or two to think about it.'

Lady Fox's formidable frontage swelled alarmingly. 'Well, really, I don't know what to say. It is most important that Roseanne should go—she is so—so countrified and gauche. Vera and Mary are so much younger and already quite self-possessed.'

Matilda, who disliked the two teenagers, agreed politely; Roseanne was dull and had no backbone worth mentioning, but at least she wasn't rude.

Lady Fox rose. 'Well, since you seem to want time to think over this splendid offer, perhaps you will let me know as soon as you have decided? Now, will you see to the post and wash the Sèvres? I have to go in to Sherborne. I shall be back for lunch—Sir Benjamin is out so there will be just myself, Roseanne and yourself. Tell Cook, will you?'

She hurried away, looking cross, and Matilda wandered off to the kitchen where she discussed lunch with Cook and had a cup of tea before going through the post.

She was in the china pantry washing the precious Sèvres china when Roseanne wandered in.

'Matilda, you will come with me, won't you? I won't go unless you do. Mother keeps on and on, if I don't go I won't stay here either, I'll run away.'

Matilda eyed her carefully. Roseanne meant it. The worm had turned, and, let loose on an uncaring world, Roseanne wouldn't stand a chance . . .

'I'll have to discuss it with Mother and Father but I don't think they would mind, just for a few weeks.'

'You'll come? Oh, Matilda, I'll never be able to thank you enough—I'll do anything . . .'

'No need,' said Matilda prosaically, 'I dare say it will be quite fun.'

Her parents raised no objection; she told Lady Fox the next day that she was willing to go with Roseanne and listened to that lady's monologue about the benefits of London to a girl like Roseanne. 'Of course *you* may not get invited to the dinner parties and dances her godmother will arrange, but I dare say you will be glad of that.'

'Why?' asked Matilda with interest.

Lady Fox went an unbecoming red. 'Oh, I have no intention of being rude, Matilda—what I mean is that you will need time to yourself occasionally and there will be no need to attend all the parties Roseanne is bound to go to. I rely upon you to see that she buys only suitable clothes, and please discourage any friendships she may strike up if the—er—young man isn't suitable. She is very young . . .'

Twenty-two wasn't all that young, thought Matilda, and it was high time Roseanne found her own feet and stood on them.

At home, she inspected her wardrobe and decided that there was no need to buy anything new. She had two evening dresses, both off the peg and by no means new, but nevertheless pretty. She had a good suit, blouses and sweaters enough, a skirt or two and a rather nice jersey dress bought in the January sales. She climbed the narrow stairs to the attic, found a rather battered case, hauled it downstairs and packed it without enthusiasm. London in the spring would come a poor second to Abner Magna.

Each day she was taken aside and lectured by Lady Fox about the London visit; she must do this and not that, young men were to be scrutinised and Roseanne wasn't to go gallivanting off . . .

Matilda forbore from pointing out that the girl was the last person on earth to gallivant, and anyway with those spots and that unfortunate nose she wasn't likely to get the chance. Let the poor girl have her fling! However timid, she was a nice girl and perhaps with her mother out of the way she might even improve enormously.

She made suitable replies to Lady Fox's remarks and that lady, looking at her, wished for the hundredth time that it could have been someone else but Matilda ffinch who was going with Roseanne; the girl was too pretty—more than that, that hair and those wide eyes weren't to be ignored. She would have to drop a word in Roseanne's godmother's ear to make sure that Matilda attended as few dances and parties as possible; no one—no man—would look at the dear girl while Matilda was there, although give the girl her due she wasn't a young woman to push herself forward; she knew her place, Lady Fox reflected, happily unaware of the superiority of the ffinches over the Foxes.

They were to travel up to London in the Foxes' Daimler driven by Gregg the chauffeur and gardener. Matilda got up early, made a tour of the rather untidy garden, ate a good breakfast and presented herself at the manor at nine o'clock sharp.

Roseanne, wearing expensive mud-brown tweeds, quite unsuitable for the time of year, looked as though she would change her mind about going at any moment; Matilda bustled her briskly into the car with the promise that they would telephone as soon as they arrived and they drove away.

It was a pleasant morning, chilly still but the sun shone and Matilda, chatting bracingly about the pleasures in store, wanted very much to get out of the car and walk or get on to her old bike and potter off for the day. She listened sympathetically to Roseanne's uncertain hopes for the next few weeks, bolstered her up with the delights of London in store for her and whenever she had a moment thought about Mr Scott-Thurlow.

The Honourable Mrs Venables lived in Kensington, in a massive red brick flat, furnished with splendour and a regrettable tendency to overdo crimson velvet, gilding wherever possible and dark, heavy furniture. She received them graciously and somewhat absent-mindedly, since she was holding a lengthy telephone conversation when they arrived. They sat while she concluded this and were then handed over to a dour-looking woman who led them down a long corridor to two rooms at its end, overlooking a narrow garden and more red brick walls.

'There's the bathroom,' they were told. 'You share it. My name's Bertha.'

'I'm not going to like it,' declared Roseanne when they were alone in her room. Her lip quivered. 'I want to go home.'

'We've only just got here,' Matilda pointed out. 'At least let's give it a try. It's all a bit strange—you'll feel better after lunch.'

She was right; Mrs Venables had a great deal to say over the meal, laying out for Roseanne's approbations the various entertainments she had arranged for her. 'We shall have a quiet evening here today,' she said, 'but tomorrow we might go shopping and there's an excellent film we might see in the evening. I shall leave you two girls to amuse yourselves during the day—there is plenty to see and do. I have arranged a dinner party or two and there are several invitations for you.' It all sounded rather fun so that when Roseanne telephoned her mother after lunch she said nothing about wanting to return home.

They spent the next day or two finding their feet. The mornings were taken up with shopping; Roseanne had plenty of money and urged by Matilda bought the clothes she had always wanted and never had the smallest chance to since her mother had always accompanied her. It was a surprise what a difference they made to her appearance, especially when Matilda, given *carte blanche* at the cosmetic counters, found a cream to disguise the spots and chose lipstick, blusher and eye-shadow and applied them to her companion's face. 'Don't you want to buy anything?' asked Roseanne. 'Clothes?'

Matilda assured her, quite untruthfully, that she didn't.

It was their third day there and they had been shopping again. It was Matilda who stopped outside an art gallery with a discreet notice, 'Exhibition Within', and suggested that they might take a look.

The gallery was a series of rooms, very elegant and half filled with viewers, and the first person Matilda saw there was Mr Scott-Thurlow.

CHAPTER TWO

MR SCOTT-THURLOW wasn't alone: there was a tall, willowy girl beside him, a fashion-plate, so slim that she might have been cut out of cardboard. She was exquisitely made up and her hair was a teased-out halo, lacquered into immobility. She was beautiful but there was no animation in her face; indeed, she looked bored, far more interested in arranging the pleats of her long skirt than viewing the large painting before which they stood.

Matilda, after the first shock of delight, wanted perversely nothing so much as to get as far away from Mr Scott-Thurlow as possible, but Roseanne had seen him too. She darted up to him and caught his sleeve.

'Fancy seeing you here, Mr Scott-Thurlow——' for once she had forgotten her shyness '—and Matilda's with me...'

He took her hand and shook it gently and his voice was kind. 'How delightful to see you again, Roseanne. Are you staying in town?' He turned to his companion. 'Rhoda, this is Roseanne Fox; we met in Dorset a few weeks ago.' He smiled at Roseanne. 'My fiancée, Rhoda Symes.'

He looked past her to where Matilda was waiting and his smile faded, indeed he looked angry but so fleetingly that watching him she decided that she had imagined it. There was nothing else to do but to join Roseanne, greet him politely and be introduced in her turn to the girl with him.

Rhoda Symes was everything that she wasn't, reflected Matilda sadly, thinking of her own pleasant plumpness and kind of knowing that in the eyes of this girl she was just plain fat, size fourteen, wearing all the wrong make-up and with the wrong-coloured hair... All the same she gave the girl a friendly smile— if she was going to make Mr Scott-Thurlow a happy man, then she, Matilda, would make the best of it; she loved him too much to think otherwise.

The girl was lovely. Matilda supposed that in all fairness if she were a man she would undoubtedly fall for all that elegant beauty.

They stood and talked for a few minutes until Matilda observed that they still had almost the whole of the exhibition to see and since Roseanne was interested hadn't they better get started?

She bade Mr Scott-Thurlow a colourless goodbye and smiled without guile at Rhoda Symes, trying not to see the very large diamond on her left hand—a hand which that lady flourished rather too prominently.

'I say,' said Roseanne excitedly, 'isn't she absolutely lovely? I wonder if we'll get asked to the wedding?' She added, not meaning to be rude, 'Not you, of course.'

Matilda, contemplating a large oil-painting which she thought privately looked as though the artist had upset his paint pots over the canvas, agreed cheerfully to this remark; wild horses wouldn't drag her to Mr Scott-Thurlow's wedding—he was, as far as she was concerned, a closed book. Or so she told herself.

Roseanne's godmother gave a dinner party on the following evening; just a few friends, the Honourable Mrs Venables had said, most of them unattached men of suitable age with a complement of safely married ladies; Roseanne must have her chance and a dinner party was a very good way of getting to know people. Matilda was to attend too although her hostess would have been happier not to have had the competition; she consoled herself with the thought that men didn't care for such bright red hair.

Matilda did her best to look inconspicuous; she did her hair in a severe french pleat, wore an unassuming gown—grey crêpe and several years out of date—and stayed in the background as much as possible. Nevertheless she attracted the attention of the company, and since she was a nice, unassuming girl the ladies of the party liked her as well as the men. She did her best to see that Roseanne was a success and her godmother had to admit that Matilda hadn't made any attempt to draw attention to herself. All the same, an excuse would have to be found for Roseanne to go without her to the dinner dance later that week, and Matilda, being told on the morning of that day that she looked poorly and perhaps it would be wise if she didn't go out that evening, agreed for Roseanne's sake that she had a very bad headache and an early night would do her the world of good.

Of course, during the days she was expected to accompany Roseanne wherever she had a fancy to go, leaving her godmother to pursue her own busy social life, and it was a day or so after the dinner dance that they found themselves in the National Gallery. It was while they were admiring some splendid examples of the Netherlandish school that the young man standing close by spoke to them, or rather to Roseanne.

'Forgive me,' he began, 'I overheard you discussing this picture—you know something about it, do you not? Are you interested in oil-paintings of that period?'

When Roseanne nodded, her beaky nose quivering with the unexpectedness of it all, he asked, 'You paint yourself?' Then when she nodded again, 'Then let me explain . . .'

Which he did at some length, taking her from one painting to the next with Matilda, intrigued, keeping discreetly in the background. He seemed all right; he had a nice open face, not good-looking, but his gaze was direct, and he had introduced himself and shaken hands. 'Bernard Stevens,' he told them, working as a picture restorer for a famous art gallery and painting when he had the time. Roseanne had to be prised away from him after half an hour or so but only after she had promised to meet him there on the following morning, ostensibly to discuss more paintings but Matilda, studying her face, thought that was only partly the reason.

'You won't tell Aunt Maud?' begged Roseanne.

'Roseanne, you're twenty-two, old enough to decide whom you want to know. Of course I shan't breathe a word.'

All the same she played discreet gooseberry the next morning, and again on the following afternoon, only now it was the Tate Gallery. She had been reassured to hear him mention the names of several people whom Roseanne's godmother had talked of from time to time and he appeared well dressed and had good manners; she was no snob, but just supposing the gentle little flirtation turned into something more serious—she would have to answer to Lady Fox.

They were to go to the theatre on the next evening, quite a small party and Matilda found herself paired off with an elderly man, a widower who told her at great length about his late wife's ill health, and during the interval, when she had hoped to escape him for a short while, he led her firmly to the bar where he fetched her a tonic and lemon without asking her what she would like. 'I don't approve of pretty young ladies drinking alcohol,' he told her and, because she had a kind heart, she accepted it nicely and sipped at it. She really needed something strong. Vodka? She had never tasted it. Brandy and soda? She looked around her—everyone there appeared to be drinking gin and tonic or champagne.

She took another sip and while appearing attentive to her companion's remarks—still about his wife too—glanced around her. There were some lovely dresses, and the grey crêpe was drowned in a sea of silks and satins. There was a vivid scarlet gown worn by someone with her back to Matilda and standing beside it, looking over the silk shoulder, was Mr Scott-Thurlow, watching her.

She went pale with the strength of her feelings at the sight of him and then blushed. It seemed impossible for her to look away but she managed it and she hadn't smiled because he had looked unsmilingly at her.

She tossed off the tonic and lent a sympathetic ear to her companion's description of his late wife's asthma, murmuring in all the right places and not really hearing a word.

She went to bed later, feeling unhappy, longing for a scarlet gown in which she might dazzle Mr Scott-Thurlow and at the same time wanting to go home then and there. She even wept a little and then her common sense came to the rescue; scarlet would look hideous with her hair and no way could she go home and leave Roseanne just as the girl was beginning to find her feet—perhaps she would find romance too.

And it seemed likely; two days later, attending a preview of an up-and-coming portrait painter and this time with their hostess, Matilda was intrigued and delighted to see Bernard Stevens. He was with a friend of Mrs Venables and naturally enough was introduced, and presently he bore Roseanne off to make a tour of the rooms while Matilda stood between the two older ladies and listened with interest while Mrs Venables asked endless questions about Mr Stevens. The answers seemed to satisfy her and Matilda reflected that their month in London would make one of them happy, at least. That night after they had gone to bed Roseanne came along to her room, brimming over with excitement. She should get excited more often, thought Matilda, sitting up in bed, lending a sympathetic ear; it added a sparkle to Roseanne's plain face; even the unfortunate nose seemed less prominent and her mouth had taken on a softer curve.

Bernard, Roseanne told her, now that he had made the acquaintance of her godmother, was going to find a way to meet her parents; her godmother was one of the few people her mother listened to, and Mrs Venables liked him. 'Isn't it wonderful?' breathed Roseanne. 'Our meeting like that? He thinks I'm pretty, only my clothes are wrong—you always said that too, didn't you? He's going to meet me one day and go with me to choose an outfit. I wish we were staying here forever.'

'Well, if you want a super wedding you'll have to go home to get ready for it, and the sooner you do that the sooner you can get married. Big weddings take an awful lot of organising.'

Which started Roseanne off again until she gave a final yawn and said goodnight, but on her way to the door she stopped. 'I'm ever so glad it's happened to me—I wish it could happen to you too.'

'Nothing,' declared Matilda in a falsely cheerful voice, 'ever happens to me.'

She was wrong; fate had a testy ear tuned in to that kind of remark.

They had been for a morning walk and now they were hurrying home as rain, threatening to be heavy, began to fall. There was a short cut to the house through narrow streets lined with small, rather shabby shops and used a great deal by drivers avoiding the main roads. They were turning into it when they saw half a dozen people standing on the edge of the pavement looking down at something.

'I'm going to see what it is,' said Matilda and despite Roseanne's peevish reluctance went to look. A small dog was lying in the gutter, wet, pitifully thin, and also obviously injured.

No one was doing anything; Matilda bent down and put out a gentle hand. 'Leave it alone, miss,' said a large untidy man roughly. ''E'll bite yer—'it by a car, 'e'll be dead in no time.'

Matilda flashed a glance at him and got on to her knees, the better to look at the little beast. It cowered and showed its teeth and then put out a tongue and licked her hand.

'How long has it been here?' she demanded.

''Arf an hour...'

'Then not one of you has done anything to help it?' She turned to look at them. 'Why, you're nothing but a bunch of heartless brutes.'

''Ere, that won't do, lady—it's only a stray, 'arf starved too.'

No one had noticed the car which drew up on the other side of the street; Mr Scott-Thurlow was beside her, bending his great height, lifting her to her feet before anyone had spoken again.

'Oh, dear, oh, dear,' he said softly, 'Miss ffinch helping lame dogs...'

'Don't you start,' she warned him fiercely. 'This poor creature's been here for half an hour and no one has lifted a finger.'

Mr Scott-Thurlow wasted no time. 'Get me a piece of cardboard,' he ordered the man nearest him, 'flat, mind you, and please be quick about it.'

The people around suddenly became helpful; suggestions filled the air, even offers of help, unspecified. The cardboard was brought back and everyone stood aside watching; they weren't unkind deliberately, only indifferent—if the big gent liked to get bitten by a dog that was going to die anyway, that was his look-out and they might as well be there to see it.

He wasn't bitten; he slid the cardboard under the dog, lifted it with the animal trembling on it and carried it across the street to his car, closely followed by Matilda and Roseanne. Matilda turned back halfway across to address the untidy man.

'Now you know what to do next time an animal gets hurt,' she told him, and added kindly, 'I dare say you didn't think, did you? Standing and looking at something that needs to be done is such a waste of time.'

She smiled at him and he smiled back, mostly because he hadn't seen green eyes like hers before.

Roseanne was already in the car, sitting in the back. 'Get inside beside me,' ordered Mr Scott-Thurlow, 'and I'll lay the cardboard on your lap.'

'A vet?' asked Matilda. The little dog looked in a bad way.

'Yes.'

He had nothing more to say until he turned into a side-street and got out. 'Stay there, I'll be back,' he told her and opened a side-door in a long brick wall. He came back almost at once with a burly, bearded man who nodded at Matilda and cast an eye over the dog.

'Let's have him in,' he suggested, and lifted the cardboard neatly off her knees. 'Coming too?'

Matilda got out of the car, but Roseanne shook her head. 'I'd rather stay here . . .'

Mr Scott-Thurlow held the door open and they went in one after the other down a long passage with the surgery at its end. 'You wait here,' the vet told her. 'I'll do an X-ray first—you can give a hand, James.'

Matilda sat in the waiting-room on a rather hard chair, cherishing the knowledge that his name was James. It suited him, though she doubted if anyone had ever called him Jimmy or even Jim. Time passed unheeded since her thoughts were entirely taken up with James Scott-Thurlow; when he joined her she looked at him mistily, shaken out of her daydreams.

'The little dog?'

'A fractured pelvis, cracked ribs, starved and very, very dirty. He'll live.'

'May he stay here? What will happen to him? Will it take long? If no one wants him I'm sure Father will let me have him . . .'

'He'll stay here until he's fit and he'll be well looked after. I should suppose he'll be fit, more or less, in a month or six weeks.' Mr Scott-Thurlow paused and then went on in a resigned voice, 'I have a Labrador who will be delighted to have a companion.'

He was rewarded by an emerald blaze of gratitude. 'Oh, how good of you; I'm not sure what kind of a dog he is but I'm certain that when he's well again you'll be proud of him.'

Mr Scott-Thurlow doubted this but forbore to mention it. 'Were you on your way back to Kensington? I'll run you there; Mrs Venables may be getting anxious.'

'Oh, I don't suppose so,' said Matilda airily. 'We may do as we please during the day, you know, unless there is some suitable young man coming to lunch. Do you know Mrs Venables?'

They had reached the door but he made no move to open it. 'I have a slight acquaintance. Rhoda knows her quite well, I believe.'

'Oh, then I expect you will be at the dinner party next week—a kind of farewell before we go back to Abner Magna.'

He had categorically refused to accompany Rhoda when she had told him of the invitation. Now, on second thoughts, he decided that he would go with her after all.

He opened the door. 'Then we shall meet again,' he said as they reached the car. Before he drove off he reached for the phone and said into it, 'I shall be half an hour late—warn everyone, will you?'

He drove off without a word, leaving Matilda guessing. Was he a barrister, defending some important client, she wondered, or someone in the banking world, making decisions about another person's money? It would be a clerk at the other end, middle-aged, rather shabby probably with a large family of growing children and a mortgage. Her imagination ran riot until he stopped outside the Kensington house, bade them a polite goodbye and drove off.

'He doesn't talk much, does he?' Roseanne wanted to know. 'I think I'm a bit—well—scared of him.'

Matilda looked at her in astonishment. 'Scared? Of him? Whatever for? I dare say he was wrapped up in some business transaction; of course he didn't want to talk. Anyway you'll change your mind next week—he's coming to your godmother's dinner party, so we shall see him then.'

She saw him before then.

The days had passed rapidly, too fast for Roseanne, not fast enough for Matilda; she wanted to go home—London, she felt, wasn't for her. True, while she was there there was always the chance that she would see Mr Scott-Thurlow, but what was the use of that when he was going to marry Rhoda? A girl who was undoubtedly beautiful, clever and wore all the right clothes regardless of expense. She and Roseanne had gone shopping, gone to more exhibitions than she could count, seen the latest films and plays and accompanied Mrs Venables on several occasions when that lady, an enthusiastic member of several committees, introduced them to their various other members, mostly middle-aged and not in the least interested in the two girls. Roseanne found them a waste of time when she might have spent it in the company of her Bernard.

There were only a few days left now and preparations for the dinner party that night were well ahead. They were finishing their breakfast, which they took alone since Mrs Venables had hers in bed, when the dining-room door was thrust open and the kitchen maid—who should have known better, as Roseanne was quick to point out—rushed up to the table.

'It's Cook—cut herself something awful and the others down at the market getting the food for tonight. Whatever shall I do?'

'My dear good girl,' began Roseanne, looking alarmingly like her mother, but she was not allowed to finish.

'I'll come and look, shall I?' suggested Matilda calmly. 'If it's very bad we can get her to the hospital, but perhaps it looks worse than it is.'

Cook was sitting at the table, her hand wrapped in a teatowel. She was a nasty green colour and moaning faintly. Matilda opened the towel gently, making soothing noises the while. There was a lot of blood, but if it was a deep cut she could tie the hand up tightly and get a taxi to the nearest hospital. Since both of her companions were on the edge of hysteria she told them bracingly to close their eyes and turned back the last of the towel. She would have liked to have closed her eyes too; Cook's first and second fingers had been neatly severed just above the second joints. Matilda gulped and hoped her breakfast would stay down.

'Milly—it is Milly?—please go and ring for a taxi. Be quick and say that it's very urgent. Then come back here.'

'Is it a bad cut?' asked Roseanne from the door. 'Should I tell Aunt Maud?'

'Presently. I'll go with Cook to the nearest hospital and perhaps you'll tell her then.' She glanced at the girl. 'Would you get a shawl or something to put round Cook?'

'There's blood everywhere,' said Roseanne, and handed over a cape hanging behind the door, carefully looking the other way.

Matilda hung on to her patience. 'Thanks. Now find a table napkin or a scarf and look sharp about it . . .'

'No one speaks to me like that,' declared Roseanne.

'Don't be silly! I dare say you'll find a cloth of some sort in that cupboard.'

Roseanne opened drawers in an aggrieved manner and came back with a small teacloth. It was fine linen and beautifully embroidered and Matilda fashioned it into some kind of a sling, draped the cloak round Cook's shaking shoulders and propelled her gently out of the kitchen across the hall and out to the waiting taxi. They left a trail of red spots across the floor and Matilda heard Milly's gasp of horror.

'The nearest hospital,' urged Matilda, supporting a half-fainting and sturdily built Cook, 'as quick as you can.'

The cabby drove well, taking short cuts, cutting corners, beating the lights by a hair's breadth. At the Casualty entrance they got out and he got out too and between them they got poor Cook in to Casualty.

There was a young man standing talking to a nurse near the door. Matilda paused by him. 'Would you please pay the cabby? I'll let you have the money as soon as I can leave Cook.'

He looked astonished, paid the man while Matilda offered hasty thanks, then took his place on the other side of Cook.

'She's cut off her fingers—two of them—they're there, inside the towel. Could someone get a doctor?'

'That's me. Casualty officer on duty. Let's have her in here.'

The place was half full, patients on chairs waiting to be seen, nurses going to and fro, several people on trolleys and a fierce-looking sister coming towards them.

'Well, what's this?' she wanted to know and with a surprising gentleness turned back the towel. She lifted Cook's arm and pressed the bell beside the couch and, when a nurse came, gave her quick instructions and then glanced at the young man.

'Shall I get her ready for Theatre? Nurse is taking a message—the quicker the better.'

Matilda was holding the other hand and Cook was clinging to it as though she would never let it go. Her skirt and blouse were ruined and her hair was coming down but she didn't give them a thought. She felt sick.

The shock of seeing Mr Scott-Thurlow in a long white coat over an excellently tailored grey suit dispelled the sickness. He was coming towards them with calm speed and fetched up beside the couch. He gave her a cool nod and she said in a wondering voice, 'Oh, I've been wondering just what you did...' and blushed scarlet as he gave a faint smile as he bent over Cook. The casualty officer was doing things—a tourniquet?—some kind of pressure so that the bleeding wasn't so bad any more and Sister was handing swabs and instruments to Mr Scott-Thurlow. Matilda, feeling sick again, looked at the curtains around the couch.

She heard him say, 'Right, we'll have her up right away, please, before I start my list. Warn Theatre, will you?' He bent over Cook. 'Don't worry too much, my dear, I'm going to stitch your fingers on again and you can stay here for a few days while they heal. Nurse is going to give you a little injection now to help the pain.' He patted her shoulder. 'You're very brave.'

He spoke to Matilda then. 'What did she have for breakfast?' he wanted to know.

'I don't know, but she would have had it quite early—about seven o'clock. She was slicing bacon with one of those machines...'

Matilda felt cold and looked green; the thought of the bacon had been too much. 'I'm going to be...'

Mr Scott-Thurlow handed her a bowl with the manner of someone offering her a hanky she might have dropped or a glass of water she had asked for. He was just in time.

There was someone beside her, a young nurse being sympathetic and helpful, and when Matilda lifted a shamed face everyone had gone.

'Don't worry,' said the nurse, 'there's somewhere where you can wait and I'll get someone to bring you a cup of tea. Mr Scott-Thurlow is going to operate at once so you'll know what's happening quite soon. Do you want to phone anybody?'

'Yes, please, only I haven't any money.'

She was led away to a rather bare room lined with benches with a kind of canteen at one end and two telephones on the wall. The nurse gave her twenty pence, patted her on the shoulder in a motherly fashion and hurried away.

She phoned Mrs Venables. 'How could she?' cried that lady in an outraged voice. 'When we have the dinner party this evening and absolutely no chance of getting a cook at such short notice. What am I to do? She must have been careless——'

'She's cut off two fingers,' said Matilda. 'I'll stay here until I know what is happening to her. She's been very brave.'

She didn't wait for Mrs Venables's reply.

She sat for an hour, revived by a cup of hot strong tea, thinking about Cook and Mr Scott-Thurlow. She shouldn't have blurted out her silly remark in Casualty—she went hot again just thinking about it—and then to have been sick . . . She wriggled with humiliation. He had been kind to Cook; she hoped that he would be able to sew the fingers back on—surgeons were clever and she supposed that he was very experienced.

The kind little nurse who had lent her the twenty pence came into the waiting-room and she got up to meet her.

'She's going to be all right,' said the nurse. 'Mr Scott-Thurlow did a good job, and her fingers will be as good as new—well, almost. He's a wizard with bones. Sister said will you arrange for Mrs Chubb's clothes—nighties and washing things and so on—to be brought in? She's to stay a few days.'

Matilda nodded. 'Yes, of course. Which ward is she in?'

'Women's Orthopaedic, second floor. You'll be able to see her.'

'I'll go and get everything now and come back as soon as I can. Thank you, you've all been awfully kind.'

She was back within the hour, Cook's necessities in a case, with a couple of paperbacks she had stopped to buy and a bunch of flowers, Mrs Venables's unfeeling, complaining voice still ringing in her ears.

'The woman will be of no use to me,' she had said impatiently. 'Now I shall have to get another cook.'

Matilda had turned a thoughtful green gaze on to her hostess. 'Has she worked for you for long?' she asked.

'Oh, years,' said Mrs Venables. 'I must say it is *most* inconvenient——'

'I dare say Cook finds it inconvenient too, and very painful.'

She had received a very cold look for that; a good thing they were going home in a few more days.

Cook was in a small ward, sitting up in bed, looking pale. Matilda put everything away in her locker, fetched a vase for the flowers and offered the paperbacks—light romantic reading which she hoped would take Cook's mind off her problems. She parried the awkward questions she was asked, skimming smoothly over the future, and invented one or two suitable messages from Mrs Venables. 'I'll pop in some time tomorrow,' she finished, 'just to see if there's anything you would like.'

'That's kind of you, miss. We all said in the kitchen what a kind young lady you were, and so very understanding.'

Matilda said goodbye and found her way out of the hospital, trying not to wish that she might meet Mr Scott-Thurlow. But of course she didn't.

She got back to the house to find Mrs Venables raging up and down the drawing-room floor while Roseanne sat in a corner looking obstinate. She had intended to spend the morning with Bernard and she had had to put him off. Her mouth was set in a thin line and she looked very like her mother.

Mrs Venables, pacing back to the door, saw Matilda. 'I've telephoned every agency I can think of,' she declared. 'There is not a decent cook to be had at a moment's notice. I am distraught.' She wrung her hands in a dramatic fashion and glared at Matilda.

'You will be relieved to know that Mrs Chubb's operation was successful and that she is comfortably in bed.' Matilda glared back. 'I can cook—I'll see to dinner this evening.'

Mrs Venables's glare turned to a melting sweetness. 'Matilda! Oh, can you really cook? I mean cordon bleu? My dear girl, however can I thank you—what a relief, you have no idea how worried I've been.' She reeled off the menu: consommé royale, poached salmon, roast duck with orange garnish and brandy, straw potatoes and a selection of vegetables, some sort of a salad—she had left that to Cook—and then peach *condé* and coffee mousse. 'Can you manage that?' She patted Matilda's arm. 'So good of you to do this for me.'

'I'm doing it for Cook,' said Matilda.

She didn't wait for Mrs Venables's outraged gasp but took herself off to the kitchen, where she explained matters to the domestic staff and sat down at the kitchen table to get organised. She had plenty of willing help, and, satisfied with the arrangements, she went away to tidy herself for lunch, an uncomfortable meal with Mrs Venables suppressing her ill temper in case Matilda should back out at the last minute, and Roseanne still sulking.

Matilda spent most of the afternoon preparing for the evening. She enjoyed cooking and she was an instinctive cook, quite ordinary food turning into delectable dishes under her capable hands. She had her tea in the kitchen, which rather upset the butler and the kitchen maid and certainly upset Bertha, who had disapproved of the whole thing to start with. 'Ladies,' she had sniffed, 'don't belong in the kitchen,' a remark to which Matilda didn't bother to reply.

Everything went well; as the first guests arrived and the butler went to admit them, Matilda gave the ducks a satisfied prod, tasted the consommé and began to make a salad. There was half an hour before dinner would be served and she enjoyed making a salad.

The Honourable Mrs Venables greeted her guests with an almost feverish eagerness. She had planned the evening carefully and if anything went wrong she would never recover from it. She cast an anxious eye over the laughing and talking people around her. Bernard had come and she sighed with relief, for Roseanne had stopped sulking at the sight of him and even looked a bit pretty. There were two more to come, Rhoda Symes and Mr Scott-Thurlow, and they entered the room at that moment. A handsome couple, she conceded; Rhoda looked magnificent, but then she always did. Mr Scott-Thurlow looked much as he usually did, rather grave; always courteous and lovely manners, though. She went forward to welcome them.

Mr Scott-Thurlow had seen Roseanne as soon as he entered the room but there was no sign of the bright head of hair he had expected to see. He listened politely to one of the guests trying to prise free advice from him while he glanced round the room. Matilda wasn't there. He caught Rhoda's eye and she smiled at him. She was looking particularly beautiful, exquisitely made up, her hair a blonde halo, her cerise dress the very latest fashion. She would make him a very suitable wife; she was a clever woman as well as attractive, completely at ease against a social background, cool and undemonstrative. The uneasy thought that her charming appearance hid a cold nature crossed his mind and he found himself wondering why he had asked her to marry him. He knew the answer to that: she made no demands upon him and appeared quite content with the lack of romance between them. He had been an only child and had lost his parents in a plane crash when he had been a small boy. He had gone to live with his grandparents, who had loved him dearly but had not known what to say to him, so he had learned to hide his loneliness and unhappiness and had grown up into a rather quiet man who seldom allowed his feelings to show, channelling his energy and interest into his work. It was his old nanny, Mrs Twigg, who kept house for him, who had begged him to find himself a wife and he had acknowledged the good sense of that; his friends were all married by now and despite his absorption in his work he was sometimes lonely.

He and the man to whom he was talking were joined by several more people and the conversation became general until they were summoned to dinner, where he sat between two young married women who flirted gently with him.

It was someone at the other end of the table who remarked loudly upon the delicious duck. 'You must have a splendid cook,' he remarked, laughing.

'I've had her for years,' declared Mrs Venables. 'She's a treasure,' and Mr Scott-Thurlow, happening to glance at Roseanne across the table, saw the look of surprised rage on her face and wondered why.

It was some time afterwards when they were all back in the drawing-room that he made his way to her side. 'Nice to see you, Roseanne, and you look charming. Is Miss ffinch ill?'

Roseanne said softly, 'No, of course not—she never is. She's in the kitchen. She cooked the dinner.' She smiled suddenly. 'We'll go and see her if you like.' Before he could answer she said loudly, 'It's rather warm—shall we go on to the balcony for a minute?'

There was a small staircase at one end of the balcony and she led the way down it and round the house and in through a side-door.

The short passage was rather dark and smelled vaguely damp. Roseanne opened the door at its end, revealing the kitchen.

Matilda was standing at the kitchen table, carving slices off a roast duck. She wasn't doing it very well and there was a large pan of rather mangled bones and bits beside her. She looked up and saw them as they went in. She was flushed and untidy and swathed in one of Mrs Chubb's aprons, many sizes too large for her, and despite that she still contrived to look beautiful. When she saw them she smiled and said, 'Oh, hello...'

'What the devil do you think you're doing?' asked Mr Scott-Thurlow with a good deal of force.

She chose to misunderstand him. 'Well, I never could carve—the bones will make splendid soup and there's still plenty of meat...'

His tone was measured. 'That is not what I meant, and you know it. Why are you working in the kitchen when you should be in the drawing-room? That abominable woman . . .' He stopped, mindful of good manners. 'Do you mean to say that she asked you to cook dinner?'

'No. I said that I would—to help Mrs Chubb; you know she was in such a state. They tell me that you did a splendid job on her fingers. Are you a consultant or something?'

'Yes. Let us keep to the point, Matilda.'

She looked meek, but her eyes sparkled because he had called her Matilda and not Miss ffinch. A tiny step forwards perhaps?

She picked up the knife again and started on the other side of the duck and he stepped forwards, took the knife from her, carved the rest of the bird with a practised hand and laid the knife down on the table.

'Is there no one to help you?'

'They're having their supper. I'll stay down here until you've all gone home.' She selected a slice of duck and popped it into her mouth.

It was Roseanne who spoke. 'Look,' she sounded worried, 'we must go back—they'll wonder where we are.'

'Very well. Have you had your dinner, Matilda?'

He looked as cross as two sticks, she thought lovingly. 'I shall take a tray up to my room. Goodnight, Mr Scott-Thurlow, or is it goodbye?'

CHAPTER THREE

MATILDA, packing the remainder of her things ready to leave in the morning, reflected sadly that it really had been goodbye and not goodnight. From upstairs at the landing window she had watched the dinner guests go home and it seemed to her that Mr Scott-Thurlow was quite devoted in his attention towards his fiancée as they left the house. Rhoda had really looked quite stunning.

She was glad to be going home; Mrs Venables had thanked her for her services rather coldly, remarking at the same time that she had no idea how she was going to manage with the temporary cook whom she had engaged. Matilda, who had been to see Mrs Chubb again, had observed rather tartly that she would appreciate Mrs Chubb's services all the more when she returned, 'Because, of course, she will be coming back here, will she not? After all these years?'

A remark which received no answer save a non-committal murmur which could have meant anything or nothing.

Gregg fetched them soon after breakfast and the two girls bade their hostess goodbye. She embraced Roseanne warmly and begged her to visit her again very soon, but when she shook Matilda's hand she observed rather distantly that she supposed that the daughter of a rector had much to occupy her and that they were unlikely to meet again.

Matilda, who had no wish to improve her acquaintance with the Honourable Mrs Venables, assured her that the likelihood of her visiting London in the foreseeable future was indeed remote.

Gregg obligingly stopped at the rectory and deposited Matilda and her case in the porch while Roseanne hung out of the car, calling to her to come up to the manor as soon as she could. 'Mother will want to know about Bernard...'

Matilda nodded and smiled, thanked Gregg and opened the door of her home to hear her mother's voice from somewhere upstairs and a moment later her father's deeper tones from his study before both parents converged in the hall to hug her warmly.

'We've missed you,' said her mother. 'It's lovely to have you back...'

'You're glad to be home?' enquired her father.

'Oh, Father, yes.' Her eyes shone with tears. 'I missed you all too.'

They went into the kitchen and presently sat down round the kitchen table to drink coffee.

'You enjoyed yourself, dear?' asked her mother. 'When you wrote and telephoned there was always a party or a dinner or something.' She added causally, 'Did you meet anyone you liked?'

Matilda cut herself a slice of the cake her mother had taken out of the oven and bit into it. She wiped the crumbs away from her mouth before she answered. 'Yes, but he's going to be married to a very beautiful woman.' She went on steadily, 'I met quite a few people I liked too but not many young ones. They went to the dances and Roseanne mostly went with her godmother.'

Her mother nodded and smiled a little; she could imagine the Honourable Mrs Venables's disquiet when she had first set eyes on Matilda—Roseanne wouldn't stand much chance...And this man? She wondered who he was and where Matilda had met him and whether he had been aware that her darling daughter had lost her heart to him. She longed to know; instead she asked, 'And Roseanne, did she have a good time too?'

'Oh, yes—we met a young man, Bernard Stevens— at one of the picture galleries, and he fell for her. Luckily he knows friends of Mrs Venables so I can't see that Lady Fox could possibly object—Roseanne wants to marry him and she can be as stubborn as a mule. He'll be down for a weekend soon, I expect, and you'll meet him or at least see him in church.'

'What a relief for Lady Fox,' observed Mrs ffinch. 'There are three daughters and those unfortunate noses... Did you enjoy the big dinner party before you left? Did the grey crêpe do?'

Matilda took another slice of cake. 'Well, I didn't go...' She paused, smiling a little, remembering Mr Scott-Thurlow's visit to the kitchen. 'The cook cut herself,' she began and recounted the happenings of that eventful day, leaving out Mr Scott-Thurlow of course.

Her mother was indignant. 'Well, really—it was one thing letting you do the cooking but she could at least have told her guests and thanked you.'

Mrs ffinch looked quite fierce and the rector said, 'Now, now, my dear, Matilda had the thanks that mattered—the poor woman with the cut hand will remember her with gratitude, while Mrs Venables is to be pitied for her lack of charity.'

His wife cast him a resigned look; sometimes she wished that he would get really annoyed about something or someone, but he never did. She smiled suddenly at him. 'You're quite right, of course—you always are.'

Matilda went to the manor the following morning to resume her usual duties there. Roseanne met her at the door and said eagerly, 'You will tell Mother what a splendid man Bernard is, won't you? She's sure to ask you. If you could persuade her to invite him for a weekend...'

'I'll do my best,' said Matilda doubtfully. Lady Fox wasn't the kind of person one could persuade easily.

As it happened her task was made easy; Lady Fox had already had a good report of Bernard from Mrs Venables. All the same she cross-questioned Matilda about him at length. 'I should like to meet this young man,' she concluded.

Matilda was catching up on the household accounts. 'I expect you have already thought of a way to do that,' she suggested. 'A weekend here would give you the opportunity to get to know him.'

'That is true, and I had of course already decided to do so. I cannot have one of my girls throwing herself away on some unsuitable young man.'

Matilda murmured. She was of the private opinion that Roseanne intended to marry the young man whether her mother approved or not.

Lady Fox got up from her desk. 'Yes, I shall certainly do so,' she said in a voice which suggested that Matilda had begged her not to.

'How very wise of you, Lady Fox,' said Matilda, looking as meek as red hair and green eyes allowed her.

Life settled back into the quiet routine which had been interrupted by their visit to London. Matilda, soothed by the comparative leisurely progress of her days, was able to think about James Scott-Thurlow in a sensible way. She was in love with him and always would be, there was no gainsaying that, but she had known her case was hopeless when she had set eyes on Rhoda. It was now just a question of forgetting him, she told herself firmly. Unfortunately she soon discovered that this was impossible.

They had been back for ten days when Bernard Stevens was invited for the weekend. Roseanne was almost sick with excitement and despair as she examined her face. 'Look at the spots,' she said pettishly. 'What am I to do?'

'I'll come early tomorrow and do your face—some of that cream you bought in London. I know your mother doesn't like you to use make-up but if I'm careful I don't think she'll notice.'

So that, when Bernard arrived, Roseanne presented a passable face to him, skilfully made up and made almost pretty because she was in love. Anyway, he wouldn't have noticed because he loved the girl . . .

Matilda made herself scarce once she had greeted him; there were the flowers to do for the dinner table that evening and then she would go home for the weekend. Not, though, before Bernard and Roseanne came looking for her.

'I've a message for you—do you remember Mr Scott-Thurlow? He asked me to say that the little dog is doing well—oh, and the cook—Mrs Chubb?—is staying with her sister and then going to a new job where there will be plenty of help.'

Matilda bent over her flowers. 'Oh, what splendid news—thank you for telling me.'

'You're awfully red,' observed Roseanne. 'It is rather hot in here.'

'I've almost finished. Are you going to show Bernard the garden?' Then she added, unable to help herself, 'I didn't know that you knew Mr Scott-Thurlow.'

'Well, I don't—just an acquaintance really. Nice chap, but I don't like that girl he's going to marry.'

Matilda stopped herself just in time from agreeing with him.

There was a splendid congregation in church that Sunday—the village knew all about Bernard Stevens by now and everyone was agog to take a look at him; he sat in the manor-house pew with Lady Fox in one of her terrible hats on one side of him and Roseanne on the other with her sisters and Sir Benjamin. He looked quite at ease and happy; presumably Lady Fox had given him her blessing, which meant that Sir Benjamin, who did what he was told, had given his too.

Going out of the church, Matilda bumped into Mrs Chump. ''Er ladyship will be pleased,' she breathed, lowering her voice since they were still in the porch. ''E looks a likely young man. Not a patch on that there friend of Dr Bramley's—now there was a gent for you, Miss Matilda. Happen 'e'll come visiting again some time.'

'Unlikely, I should think, Mrs Chump. What a lovely day it is...'

Bernard left on Monday morning and Matilda was met by an ecstatic Roseanne with the news that they were to become engaged. 'Isn't it marvellous?' she wanted to know. 'I'm going up to town tomorrow to meet him and choose the ring.' She danced away, calling as she went, 'I've been so afraid I'd get left like you and be an old maid!'

What a good start to a Monday morning, thought Matilda gloomily as she went along to Lady Fox's sitting-room and started on the post. That lady joined her almost at once and spent the next hour expressing her satisfaction at her daughter's engagement. 'Quite a good family,' she conceded of Bernard, 'related to the Crofts of Norfolk, and he has good prospects.' She glanced up from the bill she was frowning over. 'Why does the butcher send this account for the second time?'

'It wasn't paid, you said that he could wait for his money.'

Lady Fox went an unbecoming red. 'You must have misunderstood me, Matilda—see that it is paid at once.' She added, 'What a pity you can't find yourself a husband.'

Only by reminding herself that no ffinch would lower herself to answer such a vulgar remark from the inferior Fox family did Matilda manage to remain silent. It was becoming obvious to her that she would have to give up her job at the manor-house; the money was useful but there was a limit to what a girl could stand. She wasn't trained for anything but she was a good cook and she liked children; there must be something . . .

Roseanne came back the next day with a diamond ring on her finger; it wasn't as large or as brilliant as that of Mr Scott-Thurlow's fiancée, but it was worth the unstinted admiration Matilda gave it.

That evening, sitting round the supper table with her mother and father and Esme, Matilda told them that she wanted to give up her job. It was a relief that no one asked why.

Her mother answered at once, 'Yes, dear, I think that will be a good thing. Lady Fox leans on you far too heavily,' and her father nodded his head in agreement, and as for Esme she gave a crow of delight.

'They'll never get anyone to do the chores like you do, Tilly, and they'll have to pay the earth too. What are you going to do?'

'Well, I don't know, I'll have to think about it.' Matilda looked anxiously at her father, who observed placidly,

'I should miss you helping around the parish, my dear, but Esme can take your place and Hilary will be back home in a week or so and will be here until the wedding. We must put our heads together...'

So Matilda went to the manor-house with a speech carefully prepared and all the answers likely to be needed as arguments as to why she wanted to leave. She was going in through the side-door when she heard the sound of breaking glass, bumps and screams.

She ran along the passage and into the hall and saw Roseanne lying in an untidy heap at the foot of the staircase, an excellent example of the Tudor period, wide, its treads worn smooth with age. It was obvious that the girl had missed her footing and hurtled down its length, scattering the contents of a tray of china and glass as she went.

Matilda bent over her and, as she did so, Roseanne opened her eyes and started to scream. Lady Fox, who had come hurrying to see what was the matter, started to scream too and Sir Benjamin, taking his time,

joined her, only he didn't scream but swore. Various
members of the staff had arrived by now and the noise
was considerable.

'Phone Dr Bramley,' said Matilda briskly. 'Lady
Fox, please stop screaming so that we can hear where
Roseanne hurts.'

That was going to be difficult, for Roseanne was
making a great deal of noise. 'My leg!' she shouted.
'My arm! I can't bear it, I'm dying.'

'No, you're not,' said Matilda firmly. 'Try and be
quiet and tell me exactly where the pain is.'

Roseanne glared at her. 'My leg, I told you—above
my knee, of course, can't you see for yourself? And
my arm, it's my wrist . . . I'm in agony.'

Sir Benjamin, who had gone to telephone, came
back and Matilda sent him for a cushion which she
tucked carefully under Roseanne's head.

'You can't leave my poor girl like that!' bellowed
Lady Fox. 'I'll get Gregg in to lift her.'

'Lady Fox, if there are broken bones they'll be even
more broken if we move her.'

'Nonsense, I'm her mother and I know what's best
for her.' She glared at Matilda. 'You have no idea . . .'

Matilda had prudently taken up a position by
Roseanne which would fend off any efforts Lady Fox
intended to make. It wasn't much use saying anything—poor Roseanne was screaming her head off,
Sir Benjamin stood there looking useless and the
housemaid together with the cleaning lady seemed
rooted to the spot. If only Mr Scott-Thurlow were
here, thought Matilda.

Dr Bramley came instead, nodded to everyone and
got down on his knees beside Roseanne.

'No one moved her?' he asked, running gentle hands over arm and leg.

'I told them to fetch Gregg and have her carried to her room,' said Lady Fox loudly, 'but of course Matilda disobeyed me and left my poor girl lying there.'

'A very good thing too—more damage done by people moving injured people than you'd believe.' He was opening his bag and getting out a syringe. 'First we will stop the pain then she must go to hospital.'

'Certainly not, Dr Bramley. Roseanne is a sensitive girl; to be in a ward with other sick patients would do her a great deal of harm.'

He drew up an injection and gave it into a shrinking Roseanne. 'She must be X-rayed as soon as possible and the bones set by an expert.'

Sir Benjamin and Matilda spoke together. 'There's King's Hall...'

'Send her there. Matilda, go and phone for an ambulance, will you? Then pack whatever Roseanne will need for a short period there.'

Roseanne opened her eyes again. The injection was already doing its good work but she was rather vague. 'I won't go unless Matilda comes with me—and stays there.' And when no one said anything, 'You heard what I said—I won't go, I won't.'

'My darling child,' declared Lady Fox dramatically, 'of course she shall go with you. Matilda, pack her things and then pack some things for yourself—it's the least you can do.'

Matilda's eyes and hair seemed to glow with rage.

She caught the doctor's eye and he winked and nodded his head, knowing exactly how she felt. 'Please, Matilda, until Roseanne has quietened down.'

'I'll go because you asked me to,' said Matilda and marched off to phone for an ambulance.

By the time the ambulance had arrived she had packed a bag for Roseanne and gone home, packed one for herself, given a brief account of what had occurred to her mother and presented herself, outwardly calm and inwardly fuming still, at the manor-house again.

She would have liked to have flung her resignation at Lady Fox's head there and then, but Roseanne needed someone with her until her arm and leg had been put to rights. It should have been her mother, thought Matilda, casting that lady an accusing look.

Lady Fox interpreted it correctly for she said defensively, 'This has been a tremendous shock to me; my sensitive nature cannot face up to it.' She embraced a drowsy Roseanne gingerly. 'Dearest child, you will soon be better. Matilda will let me know what is to be done.'

Dr Bramley, supervising the patient's disposal in the ambulance, heard that. 'I shall phone you as soon as it's been decided what has to be done, Lady Fox, then you can make your own arrangements concerning Roseanne.'

Matilda got into the car beside him as the ambulance pulled away. 'Someone should let Bernard know,' she pointed out tartly as Dr Bramley started the car.

King's Hall was twenty minutes' drive away, a private hospital set in pleasant surroundings and with a high reputation. Roseanne was conveyed into it and taken straight to the X-ray department with no delay while Matilda sat patiently in the comfortably furnished waiting-room. Someone brought her coffee after a time and told her kindly that once the specialist had seen Roseanne someone would be along to make whatever arrangements were necessary.

Matilda drank her coffee, ate all the biscuits and speculated about lunch, and not only lunch; Lady Fox had told her to stay with Roseanne but perhaps the hospital wouldn't approve of that—perhaps she ought to phone...

There was a small stir in the hall and a moment later the half-open door of the waiting-room was thrust open. Mr Scott-Thurlow, looking calm, grave and unhurried came in.

'Ah, Matilda, I felt in my bones...' He didn't go on. 'Be good enough not to go away—I'll see you presently...'

She sat staring at him, awash with delight. She should have known—Lady Fox would have demanded the very best treatment for her daughter and he was undoubtedly the very best. Suddenly the annoyance she had felt at being sent with Roseanne melted away; fate had very kindly thrust her in his path once more, which was delightful—probably he felt no delight at all though. A pity she couldn't have thought of something to say instead of gasping at him like a stranded fish.

She heard one o'clock strike somewhere and a moment later a smartly dressed domestic came in carrying a tray which she set on a small table. She smiled at Matilda. 'Your lunch, Miss,' and hard on her heels came a dignified lady in a grey dress and a fetching muslin cap.

'They're in Theatre now,' she explained, 'and it may be some time. Please make yourself comfortable in the meantime.' She smiled and went away and

Matilda, a girl with a healthy appetite, lifted the lids covering the dishes on the tray. Soup in a pitkin, piping hot, fish and creamed potatoes, broccoli and carrots and a baked custard.

She sat herself down and ate the lot and the domestic came back with a tray of coffee just as she had finished. She went back to her easy chair then and since there was nothing else much to do she closed her eyes and dozed off.

Mr Scott-Thurlow, coming silently into the room, paused by the door. She made a delightful picture, her glorious fiery hair against the soft green of the chair in which she was sprawling. He stood for a few moments looking down at her and then bent and touched her shoulder gently.

She woke at once and smiled widely and sat up. 'Is everything all right?'

He sat down opposite her. 'Yes. Roseanne's arm is in plaster, a simple fracture which should knit quickly. Her leg is rather more complicated: a double fracture above the knee—rather unusual; it will have to be in extension for some weeks. She has come round from the anaesthetic but is asleep now. I've spoken to her mother—I gather that you are to stay here with her until such time as she feels she can cope without you.' He smiled faintly. 'An arrangement which I hope doesn't inconvenience you at all?'

'Well, as a matter of fact, it does. I was going to tell Lady Fox this morning that I wanted to leave, but before I could do that Roseanne fell down the stairs.'

'But you will stay here as long as you think it necessary?'

'I suppose so. Perhaps Lady Fox could come and stay here. I'm not necessary here; there must be plenty of nurses.'

'There are.' He looked up as Dr Bramley came into the room and sat down.

'Hello, Matilda. They're bringing tea and presently you'll be taken to see Roseanne and then shown your room. James, what had Lady Fox got to say?'

'I had to refuse her—er—request to remain here. I have patients to see this evening and a list in the morning. I'll be down again in a couple of days and we'll take another X-ray but I foresee no complications.'

Tea was brought in then and Matilda was invited to pour out.

'I've had a talk with Matron,' said Mr Scott-Thurlow, 'and explained the position with regard to you, Matilda; I'm sure that you will find her and the nurses most kind and helpful. I have also asked her to allow Bernard Stevens to visit at any time—he seems to have a great deal of influence with Roseanne.'

'Thank you. How long do you suppose I must stay here?'

He raised his eyebrows. 'That is something I am unable to tell you. It depends on Lady Fox, does it not?'

'Well, yes, of course it does. But she will listen to you because you're an—eminent surgeon.'

'I'll do my best.' He spoke gravely but she had the feeling that he was laughing silently. 'I saw Mrs Chubb this morning. She is doing excellently—she sent her love. So did that little rascal of a dog...'

'He's still at the vet?'

'For another week. Can you suggest a name for him before I introduce him to my household?'

'He was in Theobald Avenue. Could you call him that?'

This time he allowed his amusement to show. 'I don't see why not.' He glanced at his watch. 'I must go. I'll take another look at Roseanne first.'

He went away with Dr Bramley, leaving Matilda to sit and dream. They didn't come back; presently she heard voices in the hall and then the sound of cars being driven away and when a nurse came to fetch her she asked if she might telephone. 'I told Lady Fox I would let her know if Roseanne was feeling more herself. Mr Scott-Thurlow has already talked to her, hasn't he? And I'm sure Dr Bramley will go and see her. And I'd like to ring my mother, if I may. I had to leave rather suddenly...'

Roseanne was awake now and fairly free from pain. She was also irritable and tearful. 'Now I'll never get married,' she wailed, 'with a broken arm and leg.'

'I can't think why not,' said Matilda hearteningly. 'In a matter of weeks you'll be as good as new and you weren't planning to marry for a month or two, were you?'

'No. Why doesn't he come? He should be here, comforting me...'

'Well, he'd have to be told first, wouldn't he? He might be out of town; you know he travels around to various museums. He's got to get here too, you know.'

'Do I look awful?'

Matilda examined the rather cross face on the pillows. 'No, if you could smile just a little you'd look pretty. It's not so bad, you know—this is a nice cheerful place and the nurses are awfully kind, and you had Mr Scott-Thurlow to put you to rights and he's one of the best, so I've been told.'

'Who told you that?'

'Someone at the hospital where I took poor Mrs Chubb when she chopped off her fingers.'

'Oh, her... Mr Scott-Thurlow is stern, isn't he?'

'I don't know him well enough to say,' observed Matilda, rather at a loss as to what to say and relieved when a nurse came in with a basket of red roses.

'Just look at this,' she begged them. 'Here's the card.'

'Open it, Matilda,' ordered Roseanne, and added 'please' at the look of surprise she got. It was from Bernard, of course—she read the card Matilda handed to her, cried a little and then, to everyone's relief, smiled. 'He's coming to see me; he's going to stay with Mother and Father until I feel better. Now I don't mind any more—not much, anyway.'

Matilda stayed with her until supper was brought, a very small light meal because of the anaesthetic, but she ate most of it and, when a nurse came to make her ready for the night, Matilda was free to be shown her own room, next to the patient's. There was TV in one corner of it and she sat eating the supper which was brought to her, watching a film while she did so.

Lady Fox had been vague when Matilda phoned her. She would come to see Roseanne in the morning, she had said, and then they could discuss what was best to be done. 'Roseanne needs all the support she can get,' she had observed. 'Fortunately you are there with her.'

Matilda had frowned fiercely at the phone. She had said with asperity, 'I should be glad if you or one of her sisters will take over from me as quickly as possible—that is if she needs someone. I need to go back home, Lady Fox; you must realise that I have to help my father in the village.'

Lady Fox had snorted angrily. 'Surely you realise that Roseanne is more urgent than anything else.'

'Yes, I'm sure that she is, but if you feel it's so urgent that someone is here with her, should you not come yourself?'

She had put down the phone before Lady Fox had caught her outraged breath. Tomorrow, she thought as she got ready for bed, she would be sent her notice and a good thing too. It would make it awfully awkward for her father, of course, and she was sorry about that, but she was sure that Dr Bramley would back her up. She got into her comfortable bed and put out the light and a second later someone tapped on the door. A nurse came in. 'I'm so sorry, Miss ffinch, but Miss Fox is being rather difficult. Perhaps if you came...'

Matilda, muttering under her breath, went.

Morning came and with it Lady Fox, in a nasty temper too, made worse since she had had to wait until the matron was free to see her. By the time she got to Roseanne's room she was rigid with annoyance because the matron had suggested that Roseanne would do much better if she had several days quiet, without visitors.

'I am her mother,' Lady Fox had said grandly.

'In that case,' Matron had replied smoothly, 'you will wish to co-operate in every way, will you not?'

Matilda was reading one of the more gossipy newspapers to Roseanne when her mother came into the room. Her eye lighted upon it at once.

'Gutter Press!' she cried. 'How dare you read that rubbish to Roseanne?'

'It's not my cup of tea either,' agreed Matilda cheerfully, 'but it takes her mind off herself. I mean *The Times* or the *Telegraph* don't print titbits, do they?'

Lady Fox gobbled, bent to embrace her daughter, who burst into tears for no reason at all, and then sat down heavily by the bed.

The visit wasn't a success—mother and daughter were too much alike for that. Matilda, who had prudently skipped away, could hear their raised voices and presently the quiet, severe voice of the sister on duty, and later Lady Fox was ushered into her room.

'And what was all that rubbish on the phone last night?' demanded that lady. 'I must say I was amazed at your rudeness, Matilda.'

'Do please sit down,' said Matilda, 'and I wasn't rude, Lady Fox, only stating facts. Now that I have the opportunity I should like to give up my job with you. I really only stayed because of Roseanne, you know, but she will be getting married soon. Let me see, it's Thursday... I'll stay with you until Saturday week if you would like that; that gives you time to find someone to take my place.'

Her companion looked thunderstruck. 'But what am I to do? I shall never find someone who will come each day...'

Not from the village you won't, reflected Matilda naughtily—the salary Lady Fox paid was a pittance compared to other jobs. Matilda, who had been unnaturally meek for far too long, felt a surge of delight at the idea of being free from her petty chores at the manor-house. She would be free to choose what she wanted to do. Mr Scott-Thurlow's handsome features imprinted themselves behind her eyelids; what she wanted to do was marry him...

She was aware that Lady Fox was speaking rather loudly in a cross voice, to stop abruptly as the door opened once more and Dr Bramley and Dr Scott-Thurlow were ushered in.

'Interrupting a little chat?' asked Dr Bramley and winked at Matilda. 'Mr Scott-Thurlow has come to see Roseanne and then perhaps something can be arranged...'

Mr Scott-Thurlow wished Lady Fox good morning and then turned his attention to Matilda. 'Roseanne is more herself today?' he wished to know.

'Oh, yes. Rather a ragged night, though, but Bernard telephoned early this morning. He is coming down this afternoon.'

'In that case I suggest that we examine the patient.' The men went away and Matilda and Lady Fox sat without speaking until they returned.

'Quite satisfactory,' declared Mr Scott-Thurlow. 'I leave Roseanne in Dr Bramley's capable hands. I shall, of course, visit from time to time. It will be necessary to take further X-rays to monitor progress. Physiotherapy will be started as soon as possible.

He stood just inside the door and Matilda thought how distinguished and handsome he was and so sure of himself... She heaved a sigh which he noticed with amusement. That there had been some kind of disagreement was obvious—the air was thick with it. Matilda had probably spoken her mind...

He went on gravely, 'I am of the opinion that Roseanne will make better progress if she is without constant companionship. Visitors by all means, and certainly Mr Stevens should be allowed to call at any time. The nursing staff here are excellent; she will not lack for sympathetic treatment.' He went to the door. 'You must forgive me if I leave now—I have a busy day ahead of me. This is an unfortunate accident for your daughter, Lady Fox, but I can assure you that within a very short time she will be fully restored to normal health and strength.'

He bade her goodbye and turned to Matilda. 'Thank you for your help,' he said and smiled and took her hand, and was interrupted by Lady Fox.

'Your bill, Mr Scott-Thurlow...'

The eyes smiling down at Matilda became icy. 'You will receive my account from my secretary in due course, Lady Fox.'

Matilda, who had done her best on several occasions to be sympathetic to Lady Fox, and failed, felt sorry for her; Mr Scott-Thurlow's voice had been courteous and straight from the North Pole, implying delicately that there had been a breach of good taste on her part.

When he had gone and Dr Bramley had gone to speak to the sister looking after Roseanne, Lady Fox spoke. 'Well, you had better get yourself back home,' she said crossly. 'It seems you're not needed here. I shall have to come over every day, I suppose. I shall forget all this nonsense about your leaving, Matilda, and expect you tomorrow morning as usual.'

'Certainly, Lady Fox, I did say that I would stay until Saturday week, but it was no nonsense. I shall leave then.'

CHAPTER FOUR

DR BRAMLEY gave Matilda a lift back home after a stormy ten minutes with Roseanne, whose threatened hysterics at the idea of being left on her own were curtailed by Matilda's timely reminder that Bernard when he arrived to visit her would expect to see a bravely smiling girl, looking her best and wearing the lacy bed-jacket her mother had had the forethought to bring with her.

On the way back Dr Bramley asked cautiously, 'Have you and Lady Fox fallen out, Tilly? I detected a distinct coolness in the air...'

She explained. 'Anyway, it's time I found something else to do—Hilary will be home for some months and Esme's awfully good helping Father. I'd quite like to get a job not too far away from home, so that I could pop in regularly. I've no idea what. I don't suppose there are many people who want someone just to see to the post and the flowers and so on.'

'I'm given to understand that you are a splendid cook among other things. I don't doubt that something will turn up. Go and see Roseanne from time to time, won't you? She needs someone to stiffen her spine; she never could stand up to her mother. This chap she intends to marry seems nice enough.'

'Oh, he is—she's a different girl when he's with her.'

'It amazes me how love can alter a person.'

Matilda said yes, doesn't it and wondered if it had altered Rhoda Symes. She thought it unlikely. Perhaps that was because she didn't love James Scott-Thurlow, or even that he didn't love her. Wishful thinking.

She enquired after her companion's bees, a passionate hobby of his, and they were still discussing them when he stopped outside the rectory and, when invited to go in with her, followed her inside for a delayed cup of coffee.

The next ten days were a bit difficult; Matilda went to the manor-house each morning, obeying Lady Fox's beck and call without outward rancour although her feelings inside didn't bear scrutiny. Her successor had to be found—no easy task, for no one who knew Lady Fox and the miserable salary she paid was prepared to work for her.

Lady Fox was reduced to asking Matilda what to do.

'Well,' said Matilda thoughtfully, 'if you were to offer a bigger salary and advertise in the Salisbury or Yeovil papers . . . and there's room enough to offer a bed-sitting-room, free, of course.'

'Well, really,' observed Lady Fox indignantly and did so. There was one applicant, a middle-aged lady, rather stolid, who obviously would stand no nonsense, expected a good deal of free time and a month's holiday and showed not the least timidity towards Lady Fox. On the other hand, she had splendid references, a pleasant voice and manner and her typing, after Matilda's home-taught efforts, was excellent. She was engaged and Matilda sighed with relief for she had known all along that, if no one had been forthcoming to take her place, she would have felt compelled to stay until someone turned up.

She had gone to see Roseanne several times, driving herself in her father's elderly car, and found her much improved. Bernard had gone again but had promised to return each weekend and, since he had the good sense to take a pile of magazines with him, Roseanne was quite happy sitting up in bed, looking at soft furnishings, tables and chairs and the like, planning their home when they married.

Dr Bramley had been quite right, thought Matilda on her way home after a particularly cheerful visit; love worked wonders. Which thought, naturally enough, led her to Mr Scott-Thurlow.

She wished that she could see him again, but although he had been back to the hospital to see Roseanne she had never been there at the same time. Perhaps it was just as well. A job, she told herself firmly, something else to think about, new people to meet and occupy her mind.

She left Lady Fox's employ ostensibly on good terms with that lady. Her father saw a good deal of Sir Benjamin and it would never do to have ill feeling between the manor-house and the rectory. On Sunday, Miss Twisk, who had taken her place, was to be seen sitting where Roseanne usually sat in the family pew and Lady Fox, on her way out after the service, bowed graciously towards the rectory pew—on the surface at least bygones were to be bygones.

It was delightful to be free of her various little tasks at the manor-house; over the weeks she helped her mother make rhubarb jam, poked around very happily in the large untidy garden, painted one of the numerous sheds which were dotted haphazardly around and then, since the weather was warm and sunny, she embarked on the drawing-room curtains, well worn and faded. Mrs Chump had rummaged around her stock and found a dye in a pleasant shade of old rose and

Matilda set to. It was a messy business but she was pleased with the result as she hung them up to dry. Still in a serviceable pinny, she went back into the house and sat down in the kitchen to drink her coffee with her mother and Mrs Coffin. The old fashioned bell, first in the row ranged beside the dresser, disturbed their casual gossip.

'Front door, drat it,' said Mrs Coffin. 'It'll be Postie, and why 'e 'as to make such a din . . .' She got up. 'The dear knows what 'e'll be up to next.'

She went away and Matilda kicked off her sandals and lolled back in her old basket chair. She said, 'Today I shall go to Sherborne and look for a job.'

Mrs ffinch put down her coffee-mug. 'Darling, but what will you do?'

'I've no idea—something will turn up. . .' She smiled at her mother and turned round to see what Mrs Coffin had been given by the postman.

Not a parcel and not the postman either. Mr Scott-Thurlow came through the door behind Mrs Coffin, bending his handsome head so as not to knock himself out on its lintel.

Matilda, to her great annoyance, blushed at the sight of him; her mother beamed a welcome and got to her feet. 'Good morning, Mr Scott-Thurlow— you're just in time for coffee. Do sit down. Have you been over at the manor-house?'

She patted the Windsor armchair beside her and Matilda, glad of something to do, got up to get the coffee-pot from the Aga.

'You must forgive me for calling at such a time, Mrs ffinch. Yes, I called at the manor on my way back from seeing Roseanne. She is doing well now.'

He took the mug Matilda offered him and Mrs Coffin said, 'Well, I'll get on with the bedrooms, me loves,' and took herself off.

Before she left the kitchen Matilda, strangely reluctant to be with Mr Scott-Thurlow, asked, 'Do you want any help with the beds?' and had actually got out of her chair again, intent on escape, when he said quietly,

'Please don't go, Matilda; it was you I came to talk to.'

'Me?' She sat down again. 'Whatever for?'

He smiled a little, and Mrs ffinch said briskly, 'Oh, well, I must get on—such a large house, you know, always something to do...'

'Please stay, Mrs ffinch. I have a suggestion to make to Matilda. I understand that she no longer goes to the manor and I wondered if she would be interested in a temporary job—not far away—between Sherborne and Montacute. An old gentleman whose wife is in hospital for a few weeks. There is a housekeeper and plenty of help in the house but he needs companionship, someone to read to him, play cards, potter in the garden with him, listen while he talks... You would of course need to live there but there is no reason why you shouldn't come home at the weekends. There is no hard work involved but it may be dull and perhaps at times demanding. The salary...' The sum he mentioned made Matilda's eyes open wide.

'Too much,' she said roundly.

'Indeed not,' he told her seriously, 'taking into account the fact that you will have very little time to yourself save at the weekend.' He didn't smile. 'I hope that you will consider it very seriously, Matilda.'

She loved him very much, but at the same time she was aware that she was just a little in awe of him; he looked and spoke exactly how an eminent surgeon should—courteous and impersonal and remote. She had no idea what he was thinking behind that calm face. She frowned. 'When do you want to know?'

'Now.'

She looked at her mother and found that lady smiling. 'You were only saying, Tilly dear, that you were going to look for a little job in Sherborne today.' Her parent gave her a guileless look.

'How would I get there? Is there a bus? And how do I get home for the weekend?'

'You would be driven there. You drive, do you not? I believe that there is a car you might use at weekends.'

'When would this gentleman want me to go?' She looked down at her pinny. 'I've been dyeing curtains...'

Mr Scott-Thurlow, who knew nothing of dyeing curtains, let this pass.

'Tomorrow afternoon?' he suggested gently. 'Try it for a week—if you aren't happy then the matter can be arranged.' He got up. 'I must get back to town— may I pick you up about three o'clock tomorrow?'

Matilda heard herself say yes as her mother went out of the room with him. It was only as she heard the front door squeak when it was opened that she realised that she didn't know the name of her new employer. She ran through the house, swept past her mother about to shut the door and raced down the garden path to where Mr Scott-Thurlow was getting into his car. He was in it by the time she reached it and she poked her head through the window, her bright hair all over the place, her lovely face inches from his.

'His name?' she demanded urgently. 'What's his name, this old gentleman?'

He allowed himself the pleasure of studying her face before he answered. 'Scott-Thurlow—Mr Charles Scott-Thurlow. My grandfather.'

A man of reserve, not given to impulse, he kissed the face, so temptingly close, raised a hand in grave salute and drove himself away.

Matilda stood staring after the car, a prey to mixed feelings: delight, surprise—and why had he kissed her? He was engaged, wasn't he? To a beautiful woman, and what would she say if she knew? Or perhaps in her particular social circle the odd kiss didn't count for anything. But it hadn't been an odd kiss...

Mr Scott-Thurlow was having mixed feelings too. After years of knowing exactly what he wanted, and that included a suitable marriage to someone who would make no demands upon his dedicated life, run his house well and take care of the social side of his life, he was experiencing an overpowering wish to see Matilda again and as often as possible. She would wreak havoc in his orderly life, she was impulsive, quick-tempered, given to speaking her mind upon occasion and, from what he had seen of her, uncaring about her appearance.

He shot past a busload of people who waved but he didn't notice. He must uproot the girl before she became important to him... He regretted now that he had offered to drive her to his grandfather's house, reflecting with his usual honesty that he had thought the whole thing up in the first place because he had wanted to see more of her. It was true that his grand-

father was in need of company but he could have
called upon any number of suitable middle-aged ladies
to fulfil that office. He could of course take a few
days off; a change of scene would help. Perhaps
Rhoda would go with him. He viewed the idea with
no enthusiasm.

He had a list that afternoon; he thrust Matilda out
of his mind and concentrated upon pinning and
plating a shattered leg, a laminectomy for the removal
of a spinal tumour and a meniscectomy to relieve a
torn cartilage. These done to his satisfaction, he drank
the tea Theatre Sister had ready for him, bade her a
courteous good day and repaired to the consultant's
room where he found an urgent message from his secretary asking him to telephone her.

There had been a mine disaster in Spitsbergen and
he was asked to go there to advise upon several cases
which might require his particular skill. He accepted
at once and spent the rest of the day making arrangements for his registrar to take over from him, booking
a flight for the next day and then telephoning the
rectory. Mrs ffinch answered.

'You want to fetch Matilda in the morning? Of
course that's all right—she's out at the moment but
she's quite ready to leave. I'll tell her—ten o'clock?
She'll be waiting.'

Mr Scott-Thurlow put the phone down with a sigh;
circumstances, unhappy for some, had dealt with his
problem very nicely. He whistled the dogs, and with
Theobald under one arm—for he was still something
of an invalid—he walked to Regent's Park, which he
strode from end to end and then back again, much
to the dogs' delight. Despite the exercise he had little

appetite for the excellent dinner Twigg, his man, served to him.

A circumstance which made that faithful servant observe to his wife, 'It's not like him, Mavis, not like him at all. Something's up and it's nothing to do with going to Spitsbergen; he's always off here, there and everywhere and never turns a hair.'

'That Miss Symes?' suggested Mrs Twigg, who didn't like her.

He shook his bald head. 'Can't be—he was on the phone to her, saying he couldn't go to some concert or other with her, quite affable too.'

Matilda was quite ready when he arrived at the rectory the next morning. She had dressed carefully in a wide flowery skirt and a plain cotton blouse with a matching cardigan, and she had taken great pains with her hair and face. Mr Scott-Thurlow took one look at her and then wished her a coolly detached good morning. She supposed that he had had a busy time of it since she had seen him last, and at the thought blushed. She hadn't expected him to refuse the coffee her mother had ready. Pressure of work, he explained pleasantly, and ushered her out to the car without loss of time.

There was no need to go into Sherborne; country roads skirting round the north of the town took them to Mackrell Cantelo, a small village between the A303 and Yeovil and as remote as Abner Magna. Throughout the short journey Mr Scott-Thurlow had had little to say. Matilda had essayed a few remarks, to be met with pleasantly non-committal replies. She had been looking forward to the trip, longing for it, in fact, but now she felt uneasy; her companion having withdrawn behind a bland face and manner. They were almost there when she hit on the answer. He was letting her see that his interest in her was purely superficial; a chance acquaintance who most providentially could fill a needed job. The kiss had been sheer relief on his part—well, he need have no fears that she had imagined otherwise. She lapsed into a dignified silence, studying the scenery as though she had never seen it before and smouldering inwardly.

They swept through Mackrell Cantelo, turned in between stone pillars and drew up before a nice old house, eighteenth century, with stone mullioned windows and a red tiled roof and set in grounds planted with rhododendrons, ornamental trees and shrubs of all kinds and boasting a small lake to one side of the house. Mr Scott-Thurlow stopped before the front door, got out to help Matilda and crossed the gravel sweep with her beside him. He didn't ring the ancient bell-pull beside the door but opened it and without delay walked in. The lobby opened into a large square hall, very pleasant and light with a polished wood floor partly covered by Persian rugs, its walls, panelled in some light wood, hung with paintings and across which hurried a spruce middle-aged man, neatly dressed.

'Ah, Slocombe, how are you?' Mr Scott-Thurlow turned to Matilda. 'Slocombe runs the house for my grandparents and is a tower of strength. You will find him the greatest help. Slocombe, this is Miss ffinch—you already know that she will keep my grandfather company until my grandmother returns home.'

Slocombe bowed his head gravely at Matilda, who stepped forwards and offered a hand. 'I'm sure I shall be glad of your advice,' she told him and Mr Scott-

Thurlow watched the older man succumb to her friendly smile and green eyes.

'Your grandfather is waiting for you, Mr James,' said Slocombe and led the way across the hall, into a large room with windows back and front.

The old gentleman who got up as they went in must have been as big a man as his grandson when he was younger and even now, in his eighties, he was upright and remarkably handsome with a fine head of white hair and the blue eyes his grandson had inherited. Matilda, as usual, allowed her imagination to go to work; in fifty years' time James would look exactly like that, it would be their golden wedding anniversary and they would be surrounded by children and grandchildren... She was suddenly aware that both gentlemen were looking at her, wearing the same half-smile, their eyebrows tilted at exactly the same angle.

'Matilda, this is my grandfather. I'm sure you will be able to help him pass the time until my grandmother comes home again.'

Matilda shook hands with the old gentleman—she liked him at once, but of course she would; he was James's grandfather and therefore to be cherished. 'I do hope so,' she said and smiled widely.

'You'll stay for lunch, James?'

'Regretfully, no. I must be on my way—I've a plane to catch.'

Matilda had an instant and vivid picture of him boarding Concorde with Rhoda, off to some exotic island.

'Ah, yes, of course, the mine disaster in Spitsbergen. Several in your line, no doubt.'

'I fear so.' He shook his grandfather's hand. 'I'll see you when I get back.'

'Taking Rhoda with you?' asked his grandfather.

His grandson looked astounded. 'Rhoda to Spitsbergen? I doubt if she knows where it is.'

'A very beautiful woman,' observed his grandparent. 'I wish I could come with you.'

'So do I.' The two men smiled at each other and Mr Scott-Thurlow turned to Matilda, standing so quietly beside them. 'Take care of him, Matilda,' he said pleasantly and had gone before she had even nodded her head.

'Now, my dear, shall we have a drink just to get to know each other? Slocombe will have taken your things upstairs and Mrs Slocombe will take you to your room presently. A pity James couldn't stay, but of course it's quite a longish flight to Spitsbergen.'

'You said a mine disaster—is that the one I read about in the paper this morning?'

'Yes, they're well equipped there for accidents and so on, there's an excellent hospital at Ny Alesund, but when there's a disaster of any sort then they need extra help. James has been before of course. A good chap—told me when he was quite a small chap that he would be as good a surgeon as his father, and he is. Bones, of course—it runs in the family.'

Matilda sipped her sherry. 'Your wife...' she began tentatively.

'Having a prosthesis—hip joint, you know. A colleague of James's did it last week. Normally she would come home but she's an independent woman, doesn't want to be an invalid in her own home, so she will stay at the nursing home until she is fit—three weeks or so, so she tells me.' He added, 'I do miss her.'

'I'm sure you do, but how nice to look forward to having her home again in a week or two with a new hip.'

'Yes, yes. She's a keen gardener, you know, able to name every flower she's ever grown.' He sighed, 'Never got over James's father dying like that. His mother too—a nice little thing she was, and quite devoted.'

He closed his eyes and was all at once asleep and she sat there quietly, her thoughts with Mr Scott-Thurlow driving himself to the airport, going hundreds of miles at a few hours' notice because he was needed. His grandfather had called him a 'good chap', which from that rather austere gentleman was probably high praise—she thought of him in warmer terms; he was everything she had ever hoped for in a husband, only there was no chance of his being that...

'Do you play chess, Matilda?'

Mr Scott-Thurlow senior had opened his very blue eyes and was watching her.

'Me? Chess? Well, in a manner of speaking—I'm really bad at it, so my father says.'

'Splendid. I shall beat you each evening after dinner. Now tell me all about your family.'

Which she did until Slocombe came quietly into the room to remind them that lunch would be in half an hour and would Miss ffinch like to go to her room first?

Matilda was led up the curved staircase by Mrs Slocombe, stout and friendly. Her room was at the side of the house, overlooking the gardens, and was rather charmingly furnished with white-painted bed and dressing-table, an easy chair or two, a pretty little lamp table and carpeted in a soft blue, echoed in the curtains and bedspread. There were flowers and books too and a small bathroom leading from it.

'Anything you want, my love, just you ask,' said Mrs Slocombe in her soft West Country voice. 'There's Alice the housemaid lives in; she'll bring you tea in the morning. Mr Scott-Thurlow eats his breakfast early—eight o'clock sharp. Miss Symes, when she's visited here, has hers in her bed—don't like to rise before ten o'clock or thereabouts.'

'If it's all right I'd like to come down for breakfast—I'm used to getting up early. That is if Mr Scott-Thurlow won't mind.'

''E don't hold with lying in bed of a morning, miss. You come down and welcome.'

She trotted off, leaving Matilda to explore her room, hang out of the window and finally sit down at the dressing-table to tidy her person.

They both enjoyed lunch; they discussed a variety of subjects, arguing happily and at length until they parted company for the afternoon, he to take a nap in the library, she to explore the house at his invitation.

'Tea at four o'clock,' he told her. 'I enjoy my tea, and if you have nothing better to do you can go through the post for me and deal with anything that needs looking into. And we might have that game of chess . . .'

It was that evening, after he had beaten her soundly and declared that he would go to bed that he observed, 'James will be in Norway by now.'

'How will he get to Spitsbergen from there?'

'Well, he will have flown to Oslo and then taken a plane to Tromso, that's in the north, and from there he'll get a light aircraft to Spitsbergen. Or perhaps a helicopter.'

'It will be late when he gets there.'

'Or early morning. I dare say there is other stuff being flown out—tools and so on.'

'He'll be tired,' said Matilda.

The old man agreed quietly, his eyes suddenly alert, but all he said was, 'Well, I'm for bed. Do I see you at breakfast?'

'If you would like that, yes.'

'My wife has never been one to languish in bed until all hours. Until she needed to go to hospital we breakfasted together every morning. We will visit her tomorrow. I go each day in the morning. James tells me that you drive. Slocombe will be delighted, for it has upset his morning's routine having to take me there and wait to bring me back.'

'Is the hospital far away?'

He mentioned a private hospital on the road to Bath. 'Half an hour or so, and it's a good road.'

Matilda slept soundly, ate a good breakfast in the old gentleman's company and then, a little nervously, got behind the wheel of the Daimler Slocombe had brought to the door, but she soon forgot to be nervous—the car ran like a dream and the roads were quiet. At the hospital Mr Scott-Thurlow broke the silence. 'Very nice, my dear. My dear wife does not drive, but of course all young women should do so nowadays—shopping, children to school. You will find it useful when you marry.'

Matilda said bleakly, 'I don't expect to marry...'

'But you will.' He smiled at her and looked exactly like his grandson, so that her heart lurched.

Mrs Scott-Thurlow was sitting in a pleasant room full of flowers. Her husband kissed her tenderly, told her that she looked beautiful and introduced Matilda.

'Ah, yes,' said Mrs Scott-Thurlow, 'James was quite right.' She smiled brilliantly. 'He told me that you were beautiful too. My grandson, you know.' She nodded her head so that the silvery hair danced around her pretty elderly face. 'He seldom notices women. It's time he took his nose out of that hospital and looked around him...'

'I fancy he has done so,' observed her husband and Matilda, turning the knife in the wound, said brightly, 'His fiancée is very beautiful; I met her once.'

'Ah, yes—you were in London, were you not? Did you enjoy your stay there?'

'Well, it was most interesting,' began Matilda carefully, 'but I'd rather live in the country.'

A nurse brought a tray of coffee and presently Matilda sauntered out, having said that she would like to look at the garden if no one minded, leaving the two old people together.

They were a delightful pair and they were fond of their grandson, but she suspected that they shared a life which they had made their own. For a small boy who had just lost his parents that had been a barrier, and he had sensed it and never overcome it although he must have come to terms with it now that he was a man with a well-established life of his own. 'But no roots,' said Matilda, talking to herself, and since there was no one else to talk to she added, 'He needs a home and a wife and a clutch of children to warm him and that Rhoda will never do that. He'll get more and more remote because she won't expect him to be anything else, and the children, if they have any, will see him for a few minutes each day and he won't know how to talk to them, just as his grandparents didn't know how to talk to him.' She plucked a weed with a good deal of unnecessary force. 'Something must be done.'

The choice wasn't great; even if she had been an unscrupulous girl it would have been difficult to divert Mr Scott-Thurlow's affections from Rhoda, who was beautiful, amusing and shared his background. Matilda, aware that she was very pretty was none the less not conceited about it—besides, he had demonstrated clearly enough that he had absolutely no interest in her. Here she paused to mull over the kiss he had given her. It had been done on the spur of the moment; probably he had been thankful that she had agreed to stay with his grandfather... She dismissed the occurrence, although she would have like to linger over it, and returned to the vexed question of Rhoda. Perhaps if she got to know her? Persuaded her that James needed to be loved and teased a little and even annoyed a bit from time to time, made aware of the fact that there was a good life outside his working world? In ten years' time, thought Matilda unhappily, he would be so wrapped up in his world of surgery that he might just as well not have married.

She started to wander back, deep in thought. Why on earth had he decided to marry the girl? Rhoda liked a social life and, granted, she would be a splendid hostess and no doubt run his house admirably—would she like waiting up if he got called out in the evening, or getting his slippers when he got home or making sure that he had enough to eat? It would be easier if she knew more about his personal life—and Rhoda's too. 'I am an interfering busybody,' said Matilda softly to herself, 'and I want him for me not her, but I can't have him so I'd better try and help.'

A depressing thought struck her; perhaps he liked Rhoda like that, cool and undemonstrative and slightly bored—at least she had appeared so to Matilda, but who knew what she was like when she was alone with James? It was a sobering thought; perhaps she would do well to hold her tongue and forget him, but she would have to wait until Mrs Scott-Thurlow was back home again and she could go home herself and wipe him clean out of her mind.

Mr Scott-Thurlow was ready to leave. Mrs Scott-Thurlow gave her a kind smile. 'I feel so much easier in my mind now that you are at home, my dear. The Slocombes are old servants and friends but it is company my husband needs. Do let me know the moment you hear from James.'

He telephoned that evening. Matilda happened to be by the phone in the sitting-room when it rang and Mr Scott-Thurlow, unable to get out of his chair with any kind of speed, asked her to answer it.

She said, 'Yes?' in a wispy voice, sure that it was James. It was; his voice, very clear from all those miles away, sent her heart racing.

'Matilda? I should like to speak to my grandfather...'

That was that as far as she was concerned. She went out of the room once the old gentleman was settled by the phone and went upstairs to her room and hung out of the window, looking at the late spring evening. He could at least have said how are you, or even hello. She went downstairs again and out of a side-door into the garden and stayed there until Slocombe opened the french window in the drawing-room and reminded her that the drinks had been poured.

Mr Scott-Thurlow was chatty. 'What a blessing the telephone can be,' he observed happily, 'although I suppose it must be complicated between here and Spitsbergen. A clear line though. James is busy, but he expected to be. He won't be back for a week—there were some bad injuries and the hospital is full. He will be ringing again in a few days' time. I let my wife know, of course—he sent a number of messages.'

None for me, thought Matilda peevishly. Out loud she said, 'I expect it's difficult telephoning all that way. I expect Miss Symes is anxious, but I dare say there's a way in which she can phone him.' To make it sound more casual she added, 'There's a time difference, isn't there?'

'Yes. I don't imagine Rhoda will telephone him; I believe that she leads a very busy life.' His voice was dry.

'I should think she would—she is so beautiful, and attractive too.' She spoke sincerely; she didn't like Rhoda but that was no reason to be spiteful about her, especially to this nice old man who would shortly be her grandfather-in-law.

The days passed pleasantly; chess, strolls in the garden, listening to Mr Scott-Thurlow talking about every subject under the sun. Matilda found that there wasn't a dull moment. They went each day to see Mrs Scott-Thurlow, although Matilda only stayed in the room for a few minutes, tactfully absenting herself for an hour or so. She got to know the grounds of the hospital rather well and she would stroll up and down thinking about James.

She would have liked to know so much more about him but his grandfather rarely spoke of his private life and she couldn't ask. He didn't talk about Rhoda either but Matilda was after all a stranger, filling a gap until his wife returned home. That wouldn't be too long, she was told, as it was now only a question of finding a suitable nurse to stay with her for a week or so until she felt quite able to be independent.

Matilda went home at the weekend, glad to see everyone again and tell them about her job.

'Sounds cushy to me,' said Esme. 'How long will you be there?'

'Not long, another week or two at the most.'

'It will be nice to have you at home again, Tilly,' said her mother.

'Yes, Mother, but I shall find another job as soon as possible. I can ask for a reference...'

She was welcomed back warmly. 'I missed you, Matilda,' said Mr Scott-Thurlow. 'The house seemed very quiet. We seldom have visitors, you know.'

One came the very next day—Rhoda Symes!

CHAPTER FIVE

RHODA drove up in a Porsche just as they were getting ready to visit Mrs Scott-Thurlow. It was a bright red car and she wore a scarlet suede jacket over a black dress, not suitable for the country but very eye-catching. She got out of the car slowly and came towards them as they stood poised to get into the Daimler.

'Hello,' she called, 'I've been at Brooke House for the weekend and it seemed a good idea to come and see you on my way back to town.' She kissed Mr Scott-Thurlow's cheek. 'I've had a marvellous time—a pity James couldn't have been with me.' She looked at Matilda then. 'Haven't I seen you before? Of course, at that boring picture gallery with Roseanne Fox, and aren't you the girl who cooked the dinner? James told me about it—what a joke.' She turned back to the old gentleman. 'And where is Mrs Scott-Thurlow? Is she——' she nodded towards Matilda '—the new cook?'

Matilda admired Mr Scott-Thurlow's nice manners. 'My wife has had an operation; Matilda is most kindly staying here to keep me company until she is back home. Did you not know?'

'Oh, I believe James did say something about it— but I've got the most awful memory, especially about anything unpleasant.'

'Have you heard from him?'

86

'I told him not to bother to phone or write, he'll only be away for a week or so. Why he has to go to these awful God-forsaken places...! He can take his pick of all the private patients he wants in town.' She looked at the car. 'Are you going somewhere? Am I keeping you?'

'We're going to see my wife. Perhaps you would like to come along too?'

'Love to. Is she in that nice place outside Bath? A friend of mine went there to have something or other done; wildly expensive too.' She gave Mr Scott-Thurlow a charming smile. 'You tootle along, I'll follow.'

Matilda drove silently, afraid that if she spoke she might say something she would regret afterwards. She was on fire with rage and a strong wish to tear Rhoda's hair out by the roots and then take a pair of sharp scissors to that red jacket. She kept these reprehensible thoughts to herself with difficulty and was relieved when they arrived at the hospital. Mr Scott-Thurlow hadn't spoken either, only as they got out of the car he gave her an understanding smile.

The visit wasn't a success. Rhoda was charming but Matilda saw Mrs Scott-Thurlow bristle with anger when she was referred to as a poor old thing. Old she might be, but poor she certainly was not, and it was doubtful if anyone had ever dared to call her that before. She couldn't be faulted in her manner towards Rhoda; she listened to Rhoda's high and very clear voice, recounting the fun she had had over the weekend, and her plans for future entertainment. 'When James gets back I'll see that he gets out and about,' she declared. 'There are several good parties and it's months since we went to the theatre together.'

Matilda, after a decent interval, said that she would take her usual stroll in the grounds and, mindful of the old people's wish to be alone for a time, invited Rhoda to go with her.

'Whatever for? Gardens bore me unless they're spectacular—besides, whatever should we talk about?' She gave a little rippling laugh. 'Cooking?'

Matilda kept her pretty face smiling although her eyes darted green fire. 'About half an hour?' she asked, and, receiving a nod from Mr Scott-Thurlow, wandered off. Trying to walk off her temper she reflected that if Rhoda was staying for lunch she herself would have a bad headache. 'What can he see in the girl?' she asked the hospital cat, sitting in a sunny corner. 'But perhaps she never talks like that when he's with her.'

They drove back presently and Rhoda, after the briefest of goodbyes and declining coffee or lunch, shot away in the Porsche.

Mr Scott-Thurlow led the way into the house as the car disappeared into the lane and there was no mistaking his air of relief although he said nothing, merely asking her to see if Slocombe would bring them some coffee. 'I know it's almost time for lunch, but a cup would be nice. Have one with me, Matilda.'

So she sat with him, drinking first coffee and then a glass of sherry and then going in to lunch, all the while chatting about nothing in particular and never a word about Rhoda, sensing that he was upset.

The days went by, pleasantly enough. Mrs Scott-Thurlow was to return home in a week's time, accompanied by a nurse, a placid little woman who didn't fuss. She was already at the hospital and her patient liked her. She joined Matilda on her morning strolls in the grounds and they got on well together.

'I shall go home as soon as you get back with Mrs Scott-Thurlow,' said Matilda. 'I came just to keep Mr Scott-Thurlow company. I've enjoyed every minute of it too; they have been so kind and really I've had nothing to do.'

'Well, there will be precious little work for me,' Nurse Watkins said. 'A couple of weeks, perhaps less, and I'll be off again.'

'Oh, don't you work at the hospital all the time?'

'No. I work for an agency but I take Mr Scott-Thurlow's—that's the grandson's—patients. I wouldn't want to work for anyone else; he's marvellous. I've been with him for years now. He's in Spitsbergen, operating on the bone injuries from that mine disaster, but, just fancy, he found time to telephone the agency asking for me to come and look after his granny. He's a wonderful man. Have you met him?'

'Well, yes, but I don't know him well . . .'

'He's engaged, you know. To a hoity-toity piece— well, I shouldn't have said that, I dare say she's all right, just not my sort. I don't think she's his sort either, but that's neither here nor there.'

It was the following morning that Mrs Scott-Thurlow, after greeting her husband, told him to take Nurse Watkins for a walk round the grounds. 'I want to talk to Matilda—all we ever say to each other is good morning and goodbye and she will be leaving us soon.'

As the door closed behind the other two she said, 'Come and sit down here beside me, my dear. I have to thank you for being such good company for

Charles; it has been the greatest help to him during this tiresome time. I told my grandson that when he telephoned me yesterday. It was a splendid idea to ask you in the first place. He tells me that you were actually going to a job when he asked that you should come to us, and reminded me to allow you to leave just as soon as I am home again, so you must make your plans. Slocombe will drive you to your home.' She leaned over and patted Matilda's hands, lying idly in her lap. 'We shall miss you and I hope that you will visit us from time to time. And now that is settled tell me something of your family and your life.'

'There's not much to tell,' observed Matilda, and embarked on a description of life at Abner Magna while she seethed silently. James Scott-Thurlow didn't deserve to be loved—he was a nasty cold-blooded creature who, as soon as he had got what he wanted from someone, ignored them; got rid of them just as he was getting rid of her. He deserved Rhoda—in fact the girl was too good for him!

She was finishing a light-hearted account of bingo in the village hall when the others came back, and she said goodbye to Mrs Scott-Thurlow and tactfully went out to the car with Nurse Watkins.

'A very nice girl,' declared the old lady to her husband when they were alone, 'and such a charming voice and manner. I wonder what is worrying her...?'

'Worrying her? What should be? She seems content enough.'

'Yes, dear, I am sure that she's as happy as possible with you. All the same I must find out.' She added casually, 'I suppose she has met James?'

'Of course—he fixed her up with us, didn't he? Besides, I remember her saying that she had met him at some exhibition or other. Anyway, he drove her down, didn't he? So of course they've met even if that was for the first time. You can't count that exhibition—I dare say they were introduced and didn't speak. Why do you ask?'

'No reason, my dear,' said his wife airily. She bade him goodbye and, when she was alone, sat in deep thought, frowning a little.

The day came when they were to fetch Mrs Scott-Thurlow back home. The Slocombes had polished and cleaned and, with Matilda helping out, put flowers in every room, and a festive lunch had been arranged. She got into the car and drove it for the last time to the hospital. She was packed and ready to leave that very afternoon; Slocombe was to drive her home, and although she didn't want to go in the least she could see that it would be much easier for Nurse Watkins if she wasn't there. 'Too many cooks spoil the broth,' said Matilda, which wasn't quite what she meant but near enough.

They were met in the hall by the matron, looking apologetic.

'There is a slight hitch,' she began. 'Nurse Watkins had severe toothache during the night and she is even now at the dentist. I phoned just a few minutes ago and he tells me that he has taken the tooth out but recommends that she should have a day's quiet before resuming her work. Shall we keep Mrs Scott-Thurlow until tomorrow, when I'm sure that Nurse Watkins will be well enough to accompany her home, or would you be able to manage for a day?'

Mr Scott-Thurlow didn't hesitate. 'Miss ffinch here will look after my wife until Nurse Watkins can join us—we cannot disappoint her after our plans have been made.'

Matilda opened her mouth and then shut it again—there was no point in making an awkward situation more awkward—and when he turned to her and said, 'You don't mind, do you, Matilda?' she shook her head meekly and murmured that of course it didn't matter at all.

So they drove back again with Mrs Scott-Thurlow sitting in the back with her husband, so delighted to be going home again that she was on the verge of tears.

Everyone in the house came to welcome her home. She was led tenderly into the sitting-room, sat in a suitable chair, offered coffee and fussed over while the old gentleman watched with a delighted smile.

There were enough people there, Matilda decided, so she got the luggage from the boot and carried it upstairs and unpacked it and put everything away in what she hoped were the proper cupboards and drawers, and then went down to the kitchen to tell Mrs Slocombe what she had done and offer to give a hand with lunch. Mrs Scott-Thurlow was quite comfortable, talking quietly with her happy husband—they would have a lot to say to each other before they sat down to the splendid meal which Mrs Slocombe had prepared, and after that, Matilda reflected, she would suggest a little nap until teatime.

Mrs Slocombe was standing at the table beating eggs. 'There you are, miss. Madam would like to go to her room to tidy herself and won't take no for an answer...'

Matilda and the old lady went very slowly up the staircase, watched by her anxious husband from the hall. 'You see,' said Mrs Scott-Thurlow triumphantly when they reached the gallery above, 'I knew I could do it.'

All the same, Matilda persuaded her to sit down for ten minutes while she combed the pretty white hair and powdered the haughty little nose. Mrs Scott-Thurlow was impatient. 'We will go back now and sit for a few minutes, and we will have a glass of sherry, my dear.'

So they trundled downstairs, which wasn't as easy as going up had been; all the same, they reached the drawing-room safely and Matilda sat her down in the chair again.

'I would like a shawl,' said Mrs Scott-Thurlow, 'just for my shoulders. Matilda, will you go to my room and get one? There should be several in the commode drawer, and when you come back we will all have that drink.'

Matilda closed the double doors behind her and started across the hall. She had taken herself half a dozen steps when the house door was flung open and James Scott-Thurlow strode in. He saw her at once and she gave him a delighted smile and started towards him.

'What in the name of the almighty are you doing here?' he demanded, his voice as cold as the Arctic regions he had just left. 'I arranged for a nurse...'

Not even a hello, thought Matilda crossly, and however did she allow herself to fall in love with such a rude, bad-tempered man?

'Arrangements go wrong sometimes,' she told him waspishly. '"There's many a slip," you know. Nurse Watkins had to have a tooth out, and I'm to stay until she gets here tomorrow. Too bad, isn't it? But I'll go the very moment she has put a foot inside the door.'

She turned her back on him and went up the staircase. She was in the gallery before she heard the drawing-room doors open and shut.

She took as long as possible finding the shawl; she had no wish to go back to the drawing-room, but on the other hand if she didn't show herself he would think that she was feeling awkward about their meeting in the hall.

'Bother him,' she told her reflection in Mrs Scott-Thurlow's dressing-table mirror. 'I don't care if I never see him again.' Upon which heartening lie she took herself downstairs once more.

He was sitting between his grandparents but he got up when she went in. 'Ah, Matilda, come and sit down and have a glass of sherry.' He pulled a small armchair forwards for her and went to the drinks tray. 'It is most kind of you to stay until Nurse Watkins gets here. Have you had time to phone your mother?'

No one could have been more polite or easy-mannered. She accepted the sherry, muttered that yes, thank you, she had already phoned home, and lapsed into silence. Presently Slocombe came to tell them that lunch was ready and she went into the dining-room with the old gentleman behind his wife and grandson.

'Splendid to see James back, my dear. His grandmother is delighted. We must get him to tell us something of his work on Spitsbergen; I'm sure it will be most interesting. So delightful that he will be staying the night.'

Matilda agreed with him, her feelings mixed.

The conversation at table was general; the old gentleman asked about the weather in Spitsbergen, the local amenities and the scenery, but he asked no questions as to his grandson's work, nor did James mention it. Matilda, speaking when spoken to on such topics as the habitat of the wildlife there, the plants to be found and similar sidelights on life in the Arctic Circle, found it strange that no one was agog with questions about James's own life and work there. Now, if she had been at home, she reflected, just returned from some place or other, everyone would have wanted to know everything concerning her, never mind the flora and fauna. The three people at the table with her were all so polite and detached; she had no doubt that they were fond of each other but they seemed unable to show it. She wondered if they had been so detached when he was a small boy, thrust into their lives at a moment's notice, and if that was why he was so reserved. She made up her mind there and then to find out.

It would be difficult. She remembered James Scott-Thurlow's somewhat acid remarks when she had asked him rather a lot of questions in his car. He had called it a cross-examination; he wouldn't take kindly to any prying on her part.

She coaxed a rather tired old lady upstairs to have a nap when they had finished lunch and then went to her room and sat in a chair by the window. It was a splendid day and she would have liked to have gone into the garden, but she wanted to avoid Mr Scott-Thurlow: besides if he and his grandfather wanted to talk she would be a nuisance. She poked her head out into the summer sunshine and was accosted from below.

'Come on down, Matilda,' said old Mr Scott-Thurlow. 'James is going to tell me something of his stay in Spitsbergen.'

'Later perhaps?' She thought wildly for an excuse. 'Mrs Scott-Thurlow is a little unsettled; I thought I might read to her for a while.'

'A good idea. Please come down when you can.'

She withdrew her head and sat down again and since she had said that she was going to read aloud she had better go and suggest it. The old lady was sound asleep.

For the rest of that day Matilda contrived to keep in the background, and since Mrs Scott-Thurlow had had strict instructions to go to bed in good time she was able to accompany her to her room to help her to bed. This took some time so that, beyond polite regrets, neither gentleman appeared put out when she bade them goodnight and went to bed herself. It was a lovely evening—just right for a stroll in the gardens. With James Scott-Thurlow, of course; such a pity that she was forced to go to bed instead. If she had been Rhoda . . . Matilda had a very hot bath and, as pink as a lobster, got into her bed and lay listening to the drone of the men's voices coming faintly from the open windows of the drawing-room below. Old Mr Scott-Thurlow's rather slow voice, and his grandson's, deep and deliberate. She closed her eyes and slept.

It was pouring with rain when she woke in the morning, dressed and went down to the dining-room. It was barely eight o'clock and she hoped that she would be able to eat her breakfast, or at least most of it, before anyone else came down. She was doomed to disappointment—Mr Scott-Thurlow the younger was already there, reading *The Times* newspaper and consuming bacon, mushrooms and eggs. He got up when she went in, gave her a polite good morning and begged her to help herself. She noticed that he folded the paper and put it on the table beside him with a faint air of annoyance, so that she said in a voice she strove to keep amiable, 'Don't stop reading for me; I don't mind in the least.'

She poured coffee, filled a plate with bacon and egg and began to eat. There was a slight edge to her voice as she went on, 'So unfortunate that I should still be here, isn't it? I'm going immediately after I've seen to Mrs Scott-Thurlow.'

It was disconcerting when he didn't answer, and, quite reckless because she wouldn't be seeing him again, she added sharply, 'Well, has the cat got your tongue?'

He leaned back in his chair and looked her over. 'What an abominable girl you are, Matilda; I'm not surprised your hair is so fiery for you have a temper to match it.' He poured himself some more coffee. 'And why should you suppose that I should object to finding you still here?'

'The look on your face when you saw me,' she said, not beating about the bush. She glanced across at him and all her ill humour evaporated at the sight of his weary face. 'Heavens, you're worn out; was it very busy at Spitsbergen?'

His eyebrows rose. 'Why the volte-face? But yes, I was kept busy.'

'Then you should take a holiday,' said Matilda, 'and have some fun. Miss Symes was here, you know, and she said there were several parties she would take you to when you got back.'

'And is that your idea of fun?'

'Parties? No, well, I'm different, aren't I?'

She didn't hear his, 'Indeed you are.'

'I mean, I don't fit in awfully well—with your kind of people. I like dining out and dancing and going to the theatre, but there's no conversation at parties, is there? Or, if there is, I can never hear it.' She gave him an almost motherly smile. 'But I expect you will enjoy yourself.'

'I am touched by your solicitude, Matilda, but you have no need to concern yourself with my way of life.' He spoke gently in a cold voice so that she went very pink and blurted out,

'I'm interfering——'

Old Mr Scott-Thurlow coming into the room at that moment saved her from uttering whatever she had intended; she wished him good morning, murmured that she would go and see how his wife was and took herself off.

Beyond giving his grandson a good look, the old gentleman said nothing and it was James who spoke. 'The matron phoned soon after seven o'clock to say that Nurse Watkins should be here by half-past nine.'

'Good. I'll tell Slocombe to drive Matilda back.'

'No need, sir. I must call in on my way and see how my patient is getting on. She was taken to King's Hall. Matilda lives only a few miles further on—I'll drop her off.'

'Splendid. Have you told her?'

'No. Did grandmother have a good night?'

By mutual consent, they began to discuss his grandmother's health.

Nurse Watkins arrived soon after nine o'clock, by which time Matilda had got Mrs Scott-Thurlow out of her bed and into a comfortable chair while she got a bath ready and put everything in order so that she might dress. She was wondering just what she should do next when the nurse joined them and the following ten minutes were taken up with apologies, regrets and goodbyes. Mrs Scott-Thurlow put up her face for a kiss and pressed a small box into Matilda's hand. 'You have been so good, my dear, and we shall both miss you. You must come and see us again soon—and that isn't an empty remark, I really mean it. Now run along and I hope this job you're going to will be a pleasant one.'

Matilda kissed the elderly cheek, shook Nurse Watkins's hand and fetched her jacket and case from her bedroom. She still had to say goodbye to old Mr Scott-Thurlow and, although it broke her heart not to see James just once more, she was determined to avoid him.

He was in the hall with his grandfather and stood quietly by while she bade that gentleman goodbye. It was impossible to avoid him now; she gave a brief nod in his direction. 'Goodbye.'

'I'm driving you back.'

'Oh, but there's no need, thank you. Slocombe is taking me.'

He shook his head. 'No, I am——'

She didn't give up easily. 'But I saw him only a short time ago and he never said——'

'I told him not to. Come along; I have no time to waste.'

She was aware that his grandfather was standing there looking amused and at the same time thoughtful. She said with dignity, 'Very well,' gave the old gentleman a delightful smile, handed James her case with a scowl and a flash of her green eyes and marched out of the door. The Slocombes had come to wave goodbye so she changed the scowl to another smile, got into the car while her case was put in the boot and then waved until the group by the door was out of sight.

They drove for several miles without speaking until he asked, 'Still sulking, Matilda?'

'I don't sulk. I have no reason to do so.'

'Good. In that case let me talk sensibly...' He ignored her cross mutter. 'You will find your fee waiting for you at your home. What do you intend to do next?' He added, 'And don't tell me to mind my own business.'

'I had no intention of saying any such thing,' said Matilda, who had been on the point of uttering those very words. 'I have no idea what I shall do next; certainly I shall stay at home for a short time. I cannot think why you should want to know.'

'Nor can I.'

The conversation seemed to have come to an end, such as it was. But presently he said, 'Theobald should be quite recovered; he is a splendid companion for my Labrador, who mothers him relentlessly. He loves it.'

'It was kind of you to take him in,' she said stiffly.

'You have no dog of your own?'

'No. Our dog died last year. I would love to have another one, but if I get a job away from home it's hardly fair on the rest of the family.'

'And you intend to leave home?'

Now who was cross-questioning? 'I haven't decided.'

Mr Scott-Thurlow allowed a small sound to escape his lips—it could have been a chuckle or a grunt—and he said smoothly, 'I'm sure that you will find something worthwhile to do. But why not get married?' He gave her a quick sideways glance. 'I'm surprised that no man has snapped you up.'

She said fierily, 'And I am not a bargain—what a horrid thing to say.'

'Not a bargain—a prize. Once you have been tamed a little and have lost your prickles and your impulsiveness—but that, of course, is the fault of your hair——'

'If you weren't driving this car, I would box your ears—you're more than horrid, you're deliberately baiting me. I hope I never see you again.' She was being childish but she didn't care.

He went on talking just as though she hadn't spoken. 'And yet you were splendid when Mrs Chubb severed her fingers; I don't know of anyone else who would have dealt with the situation with such good sense, nor can I think of any woman I know who would have retired to the kitchen and cooked a meal to cordon bleu standard. And Theobald—you made it your business to help him and you didn't stop to think, did you? The men could have turned nasty; you had no idea what to do with him, had you? Yet you rushed to his aid—and you have been kindness itself to my grandmother and Roseanne. I am forced to the conclusion that it is I who rub you up the wrong way.'

'This is a pointless conversation, Mr Scott-Thurlow.'

She peeped at him; his profile looked grim. He had looked so tired... Her ill humour evaporated, she said,

'I'm sorry if I annoy you—you must be tired. Mother will have coffee ready; perhaps you would like a cup before you go to King's Hall?'

His stern mouth relaxed. 'Why, thank you, Matilda.'

Her mother flung the door open as the car stopped. 'There you are—how nice to see you, Mr Scott-Thurlow; come on in, both of you. There's coffee ready and I made a lardy cake.' She embraced Matilda and shook hands with Mr Scott-Thurlow. 'Dr Bramley told us that you had gone to Spitsbergen to help those poor men in that frightful accident.'

She led the way to the kitchen. 'Sit down, won't you? You don't mind having your coffee here? The sitting-room's being cleaned.'

Mr Scott-Thurlow sat down facing Matilda, made polite small talk with the rector and then said that he must go.

'I expect that you will take a little holiday,' said Mrs ffinch chattily. 'You must need a rest and a change. I dare say it's rather different at Spitsbergen.'

He agreed pleasantly. 'But I hear from Matilda that my fiancée has several parties lined up for me.' He bade her goodbye, shook the rector's hand and paused by Matilda's chair. 'I'll give Theobald your love,' he told her. 'Goodbye, Matilda.'

The rector went with him to his car and Mrs ffinch poured more coffee. 'Such a nice man,' she commented. 'He looked tired—he should go somewhere quiet for a few days but I dare say he won't get the chance; Lady Fox was telling me that his fiancée has been to visit Roseanne at the hospital and told her that she had planned dinner parties and theatres and I don't know what else; she said that he needed to be taken out of himself, whatever that means. I don't think she should be his wife—he needs someone more suitable.'

Matilda said slowly. 'But she is suitable, Mother: she comes from a similar background, she's lovely to look at and dresses marvellously and she'll be a perfect hostess . . .'

'I should have thought that what he needed was a perfect wife and mother of his children.' She saw the look on Matilda's face and went on quickly, 'Now do tell me about this nice old couple you've been staying with, and is Mrs Scott-Thurlow quite well again?'

Matilda listened to the gentle purr of the Rolls going down the drive—she would never see him again; she didn't want to believe it but it was true. She began to tell her mother about her stay. She looked unhappy but her mother pretended not to notice that. Her dear Tilly would tell her why in time, although she could guess very well who it was that had taken the happy look from her eyes. She frowned a little; Mr Scott-Thurlow had paid scant attention to Matilda—in fact he had behaved with the scrupulous civility of someone being polite at all costs towards a person they disliked. She had been very stiff too. They must have quarrelled. Somehow the thought cheered Mrs ffinch; at least they weren't indifferent to each other. He was of course engaged to marry that other girl but she dismissed that with a maternal single-mindedness. Tilly would make him a good wife. When Matilda had finished her disjointed tale, Mrs ffinch said brightly, 'There's a letter for you, Tilly. It's in the hall.'

It contained a cheque and a short businesslike note stating what it was for; it was signed 'J. Scott-

Thurlow'. Or, at least, that was what she supposed it was; it was almost unreadable.

'Isn't it funny,' she observed to her mother, 'that someone who can put bones together again is unable to write legibly?'

'Yes, dear, but we can't excel in everything. I'm told that Roseanne is doing very well. I didn't realise that he was so well-known until Lady Fox waylaid me the other day—she has a new hat, dear, tweed and floppy, quite terrible—where was I? Oh, yes—well, she kept on and on about his brilliance and then told me what his fees were for the operation on Roseanne. Not that I wanted to know; she is sometimes vulgar, you know. I must tell you something else, though; Dr Bramley told me that Mr Scott-Thurlow refuses his fees when he is asked to give his aid at some disaster. The trip to Spitsbergen must have left him very out of pocket.' She added thoughtfully, 'It's a pity that Lady Fox doesn't know that.'

She glanced at the tell-tale face Matilda turned to her and went on cheerfully, 'It's lovely to have you home again, Tilly. They missed you in Sunday school, thought I must say Esme does very well, your Father did say.'

'It's grand to be back, Mother.' Matilda studied the cheque; it was quite a nice sum of money. 'I'll pop into Sherborne tomorrow and pay this in, and at the same time I'll poke around and see if there are any jobs going.'

She had friends there but none of them knew of any likely job; she had no qualifications, but they were full of suggestions as they sat over coffee at the café opposite the abbey. None of them very practical, though; Matilda parted from them presently and went off to do some shopping for her mother. That done, she wandered into the bookshop in Cheap Street and thumbed through the magazines. The *Lady* had pages of adverts, too many to skim through in the shop. She bought a copy and took herself off to the restaurant in Denners where she sat down with a pot of tea and a plate of sandwiches and began to search the pages.

There were dozens of jobs, mostly for trained nannies and married couples, and she had nearly given up when her eye lighted on a lengthy advertisement under the heading 'Educational'. A young lady was needed for the rest of the school term—barely a month now—and the week subsequent to that, to take the place of a junior matron to work under the school matron, and to be in charge of the youngest girls—all boarders. No teaching would be required, but a sense of discipline and common sense were essential. The salary, from Matilda's point of view, was adequate, and to crown everything the school was situated in a small town north of Sherborne, a few miles on the other side of the A303, a mere matter of fifteen miles or so from her home.

Never one to beat about the bush, she gobbled her sandwich, drained the teapot and went off to find the nearest phone box.

The voice at the other end of the line sounded severe but faintly desperate. There had been several applicants but none of them had been satisfactory—the voice gave Matilda the strong impression that she wasn't expected to be satisfactory either, but she persevered. Having a rector for a father, once she disclosed this fact, was the turning-point in her favour. She was bidden to attend an interview on the following morning.

The occasion warranted recognition of some kind; she had paid her cheque into her bank account, put aside a good deal of it to give to her mother for Esme's fees, and went on an impulsive shopping spree. She didn't dare spend too much, though—probably the owner of the voice wouldn't think her good matron material—all the same she bought chocolates for Esme, tobacco for her father's pipe, a bottle of perfume for her mother and a charming little teapot from the china shop in Cheap Street for Hilary—it would do very nicely for her to use when she was married. The boys could have money—she would send it to them at school.

She bore her gifts home, told her family what she had done, handed over the presents and went to select an outfit for the interview. Something sober, she decided, suitable for a junior matron. Eyeing her rather basic wardrobe she found herself thinking about Mr Scott-Thurlow—probably at one of the parties Rhoda had lined up for him. A pity she couldn't tell him that she had found something worthwhile, and in record time. Being Matilda, of course, she never doubted that she would get the job.

CHAPTER SIX

MATILDA, soberly clad in a jacket and skirt, borrowed her father's car and drove herself to her appointment. It was for eleven o'clock and she allowed plenty of time. She knew where the school was; it was fairly well known, taking mostly boarders, children whose parents were overseas and, unlike most schools, it was for girls only.

She got there too soon and parked the car some distance from the wide gateway, thinking up suitable answers to the likely questions she might expect, but this palled after a time and she allowed herself to think of Mr Scott-Thurlow. What would he be doing? she wondered. Sitting in some handsome consulting-room, she supposed, behind an imposing desk, listening courteously to some wealthy patient complaining about his bones. On the other hand, he might be doing one of those ward rounds which always looked so impressive in films. He might even be spending the day with Rhoda...

Mr Scott-Thurlow was bending his large person over his patient on the operating table, meticulously piecing together bits of a bone in a boy's leg, wiring them together and fitting them into a whole with all the care of a jigsaw puzzle enthusiast. Unlike Matilda, he wasn't allowing his thoughts to wander...

Matilda glanced at her watch and started the car, turned in through the gates and stopped neatly in front of the front entrance of the school. It had at one time been the country estate of a member of the eighteenth-century nobility, a point stressed in the prospectus, and any necessary additions and alterations which had been done had been prudently carried out at the back of it and its imposing Georgian front had been left in its original state. Matilda got out, rang the bell and waited composedly to be admitted. The maid who came to the door was rather wooden-faced and dressed in a print frock, white apron and cap. A nice touch, thought Matilda, suitable for a school which had a high reputation for the educating of girls. She gave her name, was shown to a small room at the side of the hall, and sat down, still composed. She wasn't kept waiting long; the maid returned and led her across the hall, knocked on a door and opened it for her. The room was light, high-ceilinged and well furnished rather severely, a fitting background for the stern lady sitting behind the desk.

She didn't get up but said, 'Good morning, Miss ffinch. Please sit down.'

Matilda got to her feet fifteen minutes later—she had got the job. Her quiet answers seemed to satisfy her questioner; her references, from Dr Bramley and her godfather, who was a bishop, were impeccable. She was asked to start in two days' time and to remain until one week after the end of term. 'You must understand,' said Miss Tremble, 'that this is a temporary post only. You will have one day a week free, that is from directly after breakfast until ten o'clock. It will be one of your duties to get up at night should you be needed. There is a head matron, who will direct you in your work, and another assistant matron who looks after the older girls. Be good enough to come with me so that you may see the school.'

The classrooms were on the ground floor, hives of activity into which she wasn't taken. 'You will have nothing to do with the teaching of the girls, of course,' said Miss Tremble in a quelling voice and led the way up the handsome staircase. The dormitories were airy and comfortable, with four or six beds in each of them. 'The small girls sleep in these four rooms and your room is at the end of the corridor.'

She was shown a small, nicely furnished room with a bathroom leading from it. 'You share this with the assistant matron,' she was told, and, 'There is a small kitchenette where you make tea and coffee if you wish. Your free time will vary from day to day and you will be responsible for accompanying any child who needs to go to the dentist or doctor's surgery.'

She was led downstairs again, bidden goodbye in a voice only slightly less severe than earlier, had her hand shaken with the brisk reminder that she would be expected by ten o'clock on the second day from then, and was ushered out by the wooden-faced maid.

Matilda drove herself home, occasionally breaking into song and uttering little yelps of delight between mental calculations as to how much exactly she would earn. She would have to wait a month, of course, for her cheque and there would be only the extra week after that; all the same, it would be a useful sum. She drove the car round to the garage and went in through the kitchen door.

'Did they give you coffee?' her mother asked, shucking broad beans at the table. 'And did you get the job, Tilly?'

Matilda chucked her jacket over a chair. 'No to the coffee, and yes to the job.' She went to the Aga and fetched the coffee-pot and a mug. 'I start the day after tomorrow...'

'Sit down, darling, and tell me all about it—no, wait a minute, I'll get your father, he's in the study, and Hilary's somewhere...'

They gathered round while she told them and then sat back listening to their pleased remarks. How different from the polite talk when James had visited his grandparents; she felt sorry for him never to have had the simple pleasure of sitting in a loving family circle, knowing that everyone there was as pleased as you were, hanging on every word and then all talking at once. She mustn't think about him though. She was doing what she had said she would do, making a bid for independence. The job was temporary, but it was a first step in the right direction, and the money was three times what Lady Fox had paid her.

Hilary drove her to the school. 'Very impressive,' she observed as they arrived. 'Do you want me to wait?'

'No, love.' Matilda got her case off the back seat and stuck her head through the window. 'Thanks for bringing me. I'll phone as soon as I know when I can have a day off. Someone will have to fetch me and bring me back.'

'Oh, Max is down for the weekend to discuss the wedding—he'll come for you if you're free.'

The same maid opened the door and this time she said, 'Good morning, miss,' and when Matilda asked her name told her it was Winnie. 'And I'm to take you straight to Miss Tremble, miss.'

Matilda put her case down and, following her across the hall, went in to Miss Tremble's room. This time Miss Tremble smiled as she entered. 'I hope that you are prepared to start work at once, Miss ffinch? Winnie will take you to your room and my senior matron, Mrs Down, will tell you exactly what your daily routine will be.'

Mrs Down was comfortably middle-aged and pleased to see Matilda. 'We've been run off our feet, me and Joan—that is, Miss Willis. We're making beds, as you can see, but now that you're here I shall be free to see to the sick-bay, check the laundry and inspect the dormitories. You'll need an overall. Come with me and I'll see if I can find one to fit you.'

Matilda was a girl of noble proportions and it was only after a good deal of searching through various linen cupboards that a garment was found that fitted more or less. 'There are two, thank heaven,' breathed Mrs Down. 'They belonged to a rather stout matron we had for a time. Not that you are stout, my dear. On the contrary, you have a lovely figure—such a small waist too.'

Matilda enveloped herself in the garment, belted it firmly and was led away to inspect the dormitories, where the assistant matron was making beds on her own. She looked cross and Mrs Down said, 'Supposing you give Miss Willis a hand first? Then we'll have a cup of coffee and explain the routine to you.'

When she had gone, Miss Willis said, 'Call me Joan—what's your name?'

'Matilda, and do call me that. Do the little girls call us by our Christian names?'

'Lord, no, Miss Tremble would never allow it. This isn't a free-and-easy place—the children have to behave and there's no familiarity allowed. They're happy enough though.'

The beds made, they went downstairs to a small sitting-room next to the kitchen. 'This is our room,' said Mrs Down. 'Not that we get much time to sit in it. We're supposed to have three hours off each day but it doesn't always work out that way—we take what we can get. You get a day off, of course, but Miss Tremble won't let any of us sleep out.'

'Yes, she told me that, but I don't live very far away—Abner Magna. Someone will fetch me after breakfast and bring me back in the evening.'

'That's nice. Now, Matilda, I'll explain your work ...'

A busy day, thought Matilda, listening carefully, especially mornings and evenings, when a score of small girls would have to be readied for their day and bathed and bedded each night.

'Quite often at weekends parents come down and take them out for tea—that's allowed. We don't get our days off at weekends, by the way.'

Mrs Down bustled away and Matilda was led off to be shown the dining-room, the cloakrooms, the changing-rooms and the room where the children could play in their free time. Despite its imposing appearance and Miss Tremble's rather severe demeanour, the place seemed comfortable and homely and the girls she glimpsed looked happy as they hurried from one class to another.

After that first day she enjoyed her work. She had some twenty small girls in her care but over and above them there were a number of chores she was expected to do so that her days were filled. The food was good and her room, though small, was comfortable. She liked the little girls and they loved her; she tucked them into their beds each night, listened to their small worries, admired pictures of Mummy and Daddy, plaited hair, inspected fingernails and cuddled the tearful victims of bruises and grazed knees. At the end of a week she was given her day off and went home, fetched by Hilary. The day went too quickly—there was such a lot to talk about—and when she had exhausted her descriptions of her work at the school there was plenty of village gossip to be discussed.

'One shouldn't listen to gossip,' observed her mother, 'but one does hear things, you know... They say that Lady Fox has given the new secretary a week's notice, but I don't believe it; she looked very firmly entrenched in church last Sunday. Roseanne is still in hospital, of course. Her arm plaster is to come off next week. Lady Fox is fussing because Mr Scott-Thurlow hasn't sent in his account. I did point out that he wasn't likely to do that until Roseanne is on her feet again and he can discharge her. After all, he's not the butcher or the baker, is he?'

Matilda had gone a little pink at his name but all she said was, 'I wonder when Roseanne and Bernard are going to marry?'

'September, I believe. Dr Bramley told me that Mr Scott-Thurlow is working too hard. That fiancé of his tries to get him to go out in the evenings and spend the weekends with her friends in the country but he almost always refuses.' Mrs ffinch sighed. 'She seems so very unsuitable for him...'

'Well, he doesn't have to marry her,' said Matilda, and just for a moment her eyes shone at the thought. 'But I expect he will,' she added soberly.

Her father drove her back that evening and before she got into her bed she trod softly through the dormitories, making sure that the children were sleeping.

Only one little girl was awake. One of the youngest there, Lucy Phelps, almost seven years old, whose parents were somewhere in South America where it wasn't wise to take children. Her father was head of a medical team sent out to get a new hospital started and her mother had gone with him; they wouldn't be home again for months and Lucy was homesick.

Matilda sat down on her bed, put her on her lap and cuddled her and let her cry quietly. 'Three months will go very quickly, darling. Where are you going for your holidays?'

'To my godfather—he's nice but he's not Daddy or Mummy.'

Matilda offered a handkerchief to mop at a small red nose. 'Of course he's not, but aren't you lucky to have him? When you come back after the holidays your mummy and daddy will be coming home in just a few weeks.'

She popped the moppet back into her bed and tucked her up and bent to kiss the wet cheek.

'I like you,' said Lucy, 'I like your name too. Do they call you Tilly at home? Have you got a mummy and daddy?'

'Indeed I have; brothers and sisters too.'

'Mummy promised me that I can have a baby brother or sister when they come home. I shan't have to be a boarder then.'

'Now, that is something nice to look forward to, love. Do go to sleep now.'

The days slipped away, filled with monotonous jobs which seldom varied, but the little girls were fun, she got on well with Mrs Down and Joan and seldom saw Miss Tremble, and between them they mostly contrived to get an hour or so to themselves each day.

On her next free day she had got Hilary to drive her to King's Hall on their way home and went to see how Roseanne was getting on. Her arm was out of plaster now and she was sitting up in bed, her leg still in extension. She was pleased to see Matilda and began at once to talk about herself and Bernard. 'You see my arm is quite all right now, but I've got to stay like this for weeks until my leg's all right. Mr Scott-Thurlow says it will be perfectly sound by September so we shall get married then.' She paused to eye Matilda. 'Mother said you'd got a job at a school. Do you like it?'

'Yes, I do...'

'Are there any men there?'

'Two gardeners and an odd-job man.'

'Don't you want to get married?'

'Not to a gardener or an odd-job man. I must fly; they're expecting me at home.'

The last few days of term came and Matilda was busy packing trunks, finding lost garments, writing labels and washing small heads of hair. Mrs Down was going with the children who had a train journey. The school bus would take them to Yeovil and it was her task to get the little girls into the right trains before boarding the London train herself. Joan was to leave next, to go home to her mother in the Midlands, leaving Matilda to see that the remaining children were collected by parents before beginning on the hefty job of stripping beds, getting the dormitories ready for the maids to clean, tidying the playroom, checking that nothing had been left in drawers or cupboards and then putting out clean bed linen by each bed ready for the beds to be made up before the new term started.

'A pity you won't be here,' commented Mrs Down, 'for you've fitted in very well, Matilda, and you're a good worker, but Joyce will be back—Miss Tremble told me this morning.'

The children were excited, getting them ready for their various journeys took all her time, and it was a relief to see the busload drive off. Joan, with the two little girls she was escorting to Manchester on her way home, left next and that left a bare dozen children, waiting more or less patiently for their parents to fetch them. Most of them were older girls with whom Matilda had had little to do and they went off in ones and twos until she was left with four of the smallest, Lucy among them.

They sat on a wall in the sunshine, hardly moving because they wanted to look their best, and Matilda, sensing their impatience, started a game of 'I spy with my little eye' to keep them occupied.

A car came up the drive and one of the children rushed to meet it; that left Lucy and two sisters. Their father came next, made polite conversation for a few minutes, scooped them up and bore them off. That left Lucy.

'He's not coming...'

'Of course he is, love. Perhaps he's got to drive miles and miles to get here.' As she spoke they both heard the car and stood up expectantly.

'It's here—it's Uncle James!' screamed Lucy as the Rolls came to a quiet stop and Mr Scott-Thurlow got out. He caught the little girl in his arms and hugged her but his eyes were upon Matilda, standing there in her outsize overall, her hair, as usual, rather untidy.

They stared at each other for a long moment until Matilda said inadequately, 'Hello.'

'You do pop up in the most unexpected places,' he said, 'just when I think...' He stopped because someone else had got out of the car—Rhoda, dressed as for a garden party and quite breathtakingly lovely.

She put a gloved hand on Lucy's head. 'Don't blame your uncle because he's late—it was naughty me; I couldn't find the right clothes to wear.' She glanced across to where Matilda was standing. 'The cook—how we do keep meeting, don't we? Is this your latest job?'

Matilda took no notice. She said, 'You're Lucy's godfather...?'

He had an arm round the little girl's shoulders. 'Indeed I am. And you, Matilda, what are you?'

'A school matron—you see, I found a job.'

'Permanent?'

She was so delighted to see him that she didn't stop to think. 'No, I finish at the end of the week...'

'So you will be out of work again,' drawled Rhoda in a sugary voice.

Matilda hadn't heard her. Somehow she and Mr Scott-Thurlow were in a world of their own—not for long, she knew that; he would make some chillingly polite remark and go away again.

She wasn't sure if she could bear that, but she would have to.

'Do you know Uncle James?' piped Lucy. 'You could come and stay with us, Miss ffinch.'

Matilda saw the look on Rhoda's face; she didn't dare look at James. 'Lucy, dear, I have to be here for another week and then I'm going home, but it's very kind of you to think of it.'

Lucy wasn't to be side-tracked. 'Will you be here next term? I won't come back unless you are.'

'Listen, love, your mummy and daddy will be home again in just a few weeks after you come back here and I expect you won't need to be a boarder then.'

'You're not coming back?'

'No. I came for a week or two while Miss Tring was ill. She's better now.'

'But I'll see you again.'

The conversation had gone on long enough. Matilda gave her a hug and kissed a round pink cheek. 'Won't it be fun if we do?' she admonished.

Mr Scott-Thurlow had remained silent; now he took Lucy's hand and started towards the car. His 'goodbye, Matilda' sounded very final.

Rhoda lingered. 'All this fuss over a child—and what are you hoping to get out of it, buttering her up like that? It's nauseating.'

She had lowered her voice, but it had a piercing quality which made it possible for Lucy to hear her. James heard her too.

Matilda put her clenched hands behind her back for fear she might slap Rhoda and turned her back. She stayed like that until she heard the car's engine. She turned round then and waved and called goodbye to Lucy sitting beside her godfather.

The big house was very quiet now that everyone had gone. Miss Tremble was still there but she would be going on holiday herself on the following day and several of the domestic staff had already gone, leaving the housekeeper, one maid and the gardeners to mind the place. Matilda took herself upstairs and started the beds, glad to have something to do, trying to dismiss from her thoughts Mr Scott-Thurlow's indifference. Yet when he had got out of his car and seen her she could have sworn that he had been pleased to see her. 'Oh, well, no good moping,' muttered Matilda, bundling up sheets as though her life depended on it.

Contrary to her expectations the week went quickly; there was a lot to do but there was the odd hour when she was free to roam the gardens or even, greatly daring, sit down at the piano in the assembly hall and thump out a few tunes. The housekeeper was kind, making sure that she ate the good food she got ready and not complaining when Matilda took her cup of tea and slice of cake out into the garden, to sit under a tree.

She hadn't been paid and she was a little worried about that, but on the day before she was due to go the postman left a letter for her. Miss Tremble had written her a kind note, promising a reference if she wanted one and enclosing her cheque. Matilda sat and admired it for quite a time, thinking of all the things for which it could be used.

Hilary came for her on the last morning and she bade goodbye to the remaining staff, quite sorry to go, but once in the car, exchanging news, her regret was soon forgotten.

'Roseanne knows you're coming home today; could you bear to see her for a few minutes on our way home?'

'Yes, all right. How is she?'

'Waiting impatiently until she's on her feet again. She's having physio so it shouldn't be too long now.' She added, 'She wants you to be one of the bridesmaids.'

'Me? Oh, no—anyway, I doubt if Lady Fox will allow her to invite me to the wedding.'

At the hospital Matilda got out of the car. 'Are you coming in?'

Hilary shook her head. 'I'll give you ten minutes.'

Roseanne was in good spirits and greeted her with delight. 'Only another few weeks,' she began at once, 'then I can get up on crutches. But I don't want to go home until I'm quite well, Mother will only fuss...' She studied Matilda's face. 'You must have been working awfully hard—you're pale or sad or something.'

Matilda let that pass. 'How are the plans for the wedding going?'

Roseanne launched into a detailed and rather muddled account of the plans; the ten minutes was up but there seemed no way in which to stop her. Matilda was searching in vain for a chance to stem the flow when the door opened and Sister came in and, with her, Mr Scott-Thurlow.

Matilda said, 'Oh, lord,' and then blushed scarlet.

Mr Scott-Thurlow, never a man to dissemble, looked surprised in a manner which appeared genuine, which, considering that he had gone to a good deal of trouble to ensure that he should visit Roseanne when Matilda was with her, did him credit. He had taken a lot of trouble to engineer their meeting, suggesting to Roseanne that since Matilda would be going home that morning it would be nice if she called in. 'I'm sure whoever fetches her won't mind suggesting it,' he had said offhandedly and had left the rest to kindly fate, telling himself that he only wished to see Matilda in order to let her know about Lucy and Theobald.

His 'good morning' was suave; he said politely, 'There is no need to leave the room; I merely wish to tell Roseanne that her latest X-ray is most satis-factory. I think we might start the crutches at the end of next week.'

He waited while Roseanne enjoyed an outburst of delight. 'You'll be here?' she asked anxiously.

'Yes, and I shall bring Dr Bramley with me.' He gave her a kindly smile and looked at Matilda, who was quite pale now. 'You have finished at the school?' he asked blandly.

'Yes.'

His small, mocking smile annoyed her, and she wished that she could think of something clever to say to him but she couldn't. Instead she told Roseanne that she really had to be going. 'Hilary's waiting in the car and they are expecting me at home.' She con-jured up a smile. 'I'm so glad you're doing so well.'

'You'll come again?'

'Oh, yes, of course. Goodbye.'

She said goodbye to Sister too and, since there was no way of avoiding Mr Scott-Thurlow's elegant bulk leaning in front of the door, she made her farewells to him too. She looked him in the eye as she did so but most annoyingly he had dropped the lids over his eyes and, since his face still wore its bland, pleasant mask, she was unable to discover what he was thinking. Why am I worrying? she mused as she made her way out to the car. He isn't thinking about me, anyway.

She was wrong of course.

'Mr Scott-Thurlow's here,' Hilary told her unnecessarily as she got into the car.

'Yes, I saw him.' Matilda busied herself with her safety-belt and her sister gave her downbent head a thoughtful look. There had been a forlorn note in

Matilda's voice. She decided not to pursue the subject and began to talk about her own forthcoming wedding.

At home, once more, Matilda was engulfed in her family; the boys were on holiday, so was Esme, and the house was full. There was no question of a holiday of course although later on in the autumn, when the younger ones were back at school, her father and mother would be going to a small seaside town in Cornwall, exchanging with the vicar of the parish there for two weeks, and shortly Hilary would be going to stay with her future in-laws again.

'Have you any plans?' asked her mother. 'There's your Aunt Penelope, she would love to have you, and you've enough money to enjoy yourself there.'

'I'll think about it,' Matilda told her, anxious to put her parent's mind at rest and not disclose that most of her cheque had been given to her. 'It's nice just being at home.'

She was sitting outside the back door stringing beans with Nelson on her lap. It wasn't very convenient but he had insisted on climbing up, pleased to see her back home again.

'Well, dear, you do just what you want—only it's rather dull for you.'

'Never dull, Mother dear. But I did enjoy that job at the school and I think I'll see if I can get something similar for the autumn term. There are dozens of schools around this part of the world.'

Her mother glanced at her. She was such a lovely girl, and nice-natured into the bargain; true, she had a temper when roused and she was impulsive, but her heart was warm; there must be a man somewhere in the world who would want her for his wife. A pity the world was such a large place and Abner Magna was so remote. Mrs ffinch cast a mental eye over the village; there wasn't a man around who would do for Matilda. Only Mr Scott-Thurlow, and that was a closed book never to be opened.

Matilda found plenty to do now that she was home again; doing the flowers in the church, taking over a class in Sunday school, driving her father around the parish, which was a scattered one, helping in the house and taking her mother into Sherborne to shop, but there was still time to wander off into the country around, sometimes with Esme but more often than not alone.

Two weeks went by, and Matilda, despite her hidden unhappiness, became nicely tanned, which made her eyes greener than ever and her hair even more fiery. She had a sprinkling of freckles too which did nothing to detract from her prettiness, and only when she was alone did she allow her charming mouth to droop and then not for long. She had plenty of good sense; crying for the moon wasn't going to help but a job would. She went into Sherborne to an agency and put her name on their books, and scanned the local paper each week as well as her father's *Telegraph*. Something would turn up, Esme assured her, coming upon her poring over the vacancies column.

It did, the very next day, in the elegant shape of Mr Scott-Thurlow, getting out of his car with the air of a man who knew what he wanted and intended to get it. Matilda was on her knees, grubbing up weeds from the rose-bed under the drawing-room windows, and since she hadn't intended to go out that day she had tied her hair back with a ribbon and put on a wide cotton skirt and a sleeveless top, neither of them either new or fashionable. All the same she looked delightful.

Esme, perched on the steps outside the french window, saw him first. She went dancing to meet him. 'Look who's here,' she called, 'just in time for coffee.'

Matilda turned to look over her shoulder. Mr Scott-Thurlow was strolling towards her. He had abandoned the drive and was crossing the lawn with Esme skipping beside him. She sat back on her heels and waited until he had paused beside her, looming above her head so that she got to her feet quickly. She had become rather pink in the face but her 'good morning' was cool and faintly questioning.

He smiled down at her. 'Good morning, Matilda. I have come to ask a favour of you. Can you spare the time to listen to me?'

She dusted the earth off her hands. 'Of course. Won't you have some coffee? Mother is indoors...'

She led the way into the house, going through the french window into the drawing-room. 'Do sit down,' she said in what Esme called her hostess voice. 'I'll fetch some coffee and tell Mother.'

'Er—might I not have my coffee in the kitchen, if your mother is busy? What I have to say is for everyone to hear.'

Her already warm cheeks glowed. He had made it sound as though she was expecting to have a tête-à-tête with him. The very last thing she wanted, she reminded herself.

Esme had gone ahead, and Matilda opened the drawing-room door without a word and ushered him through, but he paused in the doorway. 'It would be so much easier if we were on a friendlier footing,' he said blandly, and at her indignant little snort, 'Yes,

I know I have not given you reason to be friendly, have I? But if you could believe that what I am going to ask of you is not for myself?'

She looked at him then. He appeared severe and remote, but then he smiled slowly, his eyebrows raised.

'All right,' said Matilda gruffly and opened the kitchen door.

Mrs ffinch had the coffee-mugs on the table; a cake, warm from the oven, sat fragrantly on a plate at its centre and in some mysterious fashion the two boys, her father and Mrs Coffin, unnecessarily busy at the sink, were all there with her mother and Esme. Mr Scott-Thurlow was welcomed with what Matilda considered to be unnecessary warmth, bidden to sit down and offered coffee and a slice of the cake while everyone else arranged themselves around the table. He was allowed to drink some coffee and take a bite of the cake before Mrs ffinch said, 'Esme says you want Matilda to do you a favour. Perhaps you would rather talk to her alone after we have had our coffee.'

'There is no need for that, Mrs ffinch. She may wish to discuss what I have to ask of her with you and it will save time if you are told at the same time.'

'Is there such a hurry?' asked Matilda sharply.

'I am going to see Roseanne, and I should like my answer when I come back, in about an hour.'

'What do you want?'

'Not what I want, Matilda,' he corrected her quietly. 'It is what Lucy wants.' He waited while Mrs ffinch refilled his mug. 'She has the mumps and very severely too. My housekeeper, who was also my nanny, is getting on a bit and although she is wonderfully kind and helpful she is tired. Lucy wants you, Matilda— no one else will do save her mother, and that isn't possible as you know. Would you consider coming for a few weeks? There is very little nursing and you will probably be bored but the child is so unhappy...'

'Well, of course I'll come if she wants me.' Matilda spoke impulsively as she so often did and then had second thoughts. 'But wouldn't your fiancée feel— well, perhaps she would rather be with Lucy?'

His 'no' was decisive and made it difficult to pursue the matter.

'Poor little girl,' said Mrs ffinch, 'of course she misses her mother, though I'm sure you do your best, Mr Scott-Thurlow.'

She glanced at her daughter, who frowned heavily and looked at the faces round the table. They all expected her to accept—somehow he had got them all on his side. She said crossly, 'Oh, very well, I'll come, just until Lucy is feeling better.'

'I wouldn't dream of keeping you a moment longer,' said Mr Scott-Thurlow. 'I know that she will be delighted. Now I must go. Could you be ready in just over an hour?'

'I haven't much choice, have I?' She was being rude and she didn't care.

When he had gone her father said mildly, 'You were rather ungracious, Tilly; he is after all doing his best for the child.'

Her mother added, 'Such a kind man, too.'

'Mother!' said Matilda fiercely, and rushed out of the room.

CHAPTER SEVEN

'I DON'T even know where he lives,' grumbled Matilda, flinging things into her case.

'Well, we can ask when he comes back.' Esme was sitting on the bed eating biscuits out of a tin and advising Matilda on what to pack. 'Don't put that old thing in,' she warned, 'it's only fit for the jumble. Take that flowery skirt and lots of tops. Will you have to do your own washing? I wonder what his house happens to be like. I know he's got a housekeeper, but lots of quite poor people have one—she's his nanny anyway, I dare say she lives there and looks after him in return for a home. She'll have her OAP anyway...'

'How you do run on,' said Matilda, who had been wondering the same thing. 'Shall I take the green dress?'

'Yes—you won't need to dress up if you have your meals with him, but if he has people to dinner or drinks you'll have to look decent. Can't you get another dress? I suppose you gave most of your wages to Mother—she'll let you have them back——'

'Certainly not. I don't expect to lead a social life, love, but I'll pack the green thing if you think I should.' She burrowed into her wardrobe. 'I'd better wear the patterned blouse and skirt.' She glanced at the clock on the mantelpiece. 'Oh, lord, he'll be here in ten minutes. Shut this case for me, there's a dear, and I'll get changed.'

She was thrusting pins into a severe French pleat when Esme asked, 'Do you suppose that Rhoda will be there? In his house...?'

'Probably,' said Matilda thickly through the pins. 'She is going to marry him after all.' It hurt to say that.

'I mean, does she live there?'

Matilda withdrew the pins from her mouth the better to speak clearly. 'I think it is very unlikely. Doctors and the like have to think of their reputations.'

'You'll be living there with him, though,' went on Esme, never one to mince matters.

'I shall be employed by Mr Scott-Thurlow, and that's quite different.'

'Why? I can't see...' Luckily she paused when she heard the car coming up the drive. 'He's here—I'll take your case. Come along, do, you can't keep him waiting.' As they went downstairs she hissed, 'Is he going to pay you?'

'I suppose so.'

'How much?'

Matilda quelled her with a frown and crossed the hall to where Mr Scott-Thurlow stood talking to her father and mother.

'You will want to know where you're going,' he observed in the mildest of tones. 'Lucy is in London with me at present, and as soon as she is well enough I thought you might go, the pair of you, to a cottage I have near Dartmouth—Stoke Fleming—the sea air will do her good.'

It would be more than two hundred miles from London, reflected Matilda. 'It sounds a splendid idea,' she said quietly. 'Whereabouts in London, Mr Scott-Thurlow?'

'Near Piccadilly and Oxford Street. Just off Orchard Street.'

'Isn't that near Wigmore Street?'

'Yes. Fifteen Blenheim Street. Your father has the address and the phone number.'

The rector nodded. 'We shall no doubt hear from Matilda once she has settled in. I hope that she will be of assistance to you and that the little girl will get well quickly.'

Everyone had gathered in the hall by now and Matilda began a round of goodbyes while Mr Scott-Thurlow shook her parents' hands and then waited patiently while she embraced her mother and father.

She twisted round in her seat to wave goodbye as they drove away and said with a snap, 'You're always in such a hurry.' She shot him a cross look and he said gravely, 'I'm sorry about that, Matilda. I promise you that I won't badger you once you are installed and I'll send you down to Stoke Fleming just as soon as Lucy is fit to travel.'

Why not? she thought unhappily, he—and certainly Rhoda—wouldn't want them at his London home. He was doubtless a good godfather and anxious to do his best for the child, but he had his work and more than that he had Rhoda.

He was silent for a while but presently he began to tell her about Lucy. 'She feels wretched, her throat is sore and she is feverish and cross, and above all she misses her father and mother. I'm hoping that you will be able to fill that gap to some extent. She seems very attached.'

The car phone interrupted him and he slowed his speed. He listened for what seemed to Matilda to be a long time, then said, 'I shall be an hour late, Henry. Let Theatre know and if possible get on with that last case yourself. The tendon. How's that boy? Good, I'll see him before I go to Theatre—be around, will you? Goodbye.'

'What boy?' asked Matilda, who liked to know things.

'A nice lad with a fractured spine; he was knocked down by a car last night——'

'Last night? You operated in the night and then drove down here to Roseanne and—and us?'

'Driving is very soothing,' he said smoothly.

'You ought to be in your bed.'

'I don't need a great deal of sleep and I promise I won't doze off over the wheel.'

'I am not in the least nervous, Mr Scott-Thurlow.'

'I suppose it's no use asking you to call me James?'

'No use at all...'

'May I know why?' He was driving fast along the A303 and despite the good weather the traffic was thin.

When she didn't answer he said, 'Ah, well, it is of little consequence.'

He drove on for a time and neither of them spoke. Presently he said, 'I'm afraid there isn't time to stop for lunch on the way—Mavis will have something for you when we get in. You must forgive me if I go straight on to the hospital. Perhaps we can talk this evening when I get home.'

'Very well.' She added impulsively, 'I do hope someone sees that you have something to eat when you get there. You can't work on an empty stomach.'

He forbore from telling her how many times he had done just that and had hardly been aware of it. 'My theatre sister takes good care of me,' he said carelessly.

She sat quietly, watching the countryside flash by now that they were on the motorway, and now and again she stole a glance at his profile, very calm and rather stern, and at his large, well-kept hands resting lightly on the wheel. Her feelings were mixed; she longed for the drive to go on forever and at the same time wished it were over.

He slowed the car as they reached the suburbs, weaving his way through narrow streets until he came out into Millbank, then Whitehall, Trafalgar Square and thence into Pall Mall and St James's Street and so at last to Orchard Street and the narrow street leading off it. Blenheim Street was a cul-de-sac with what looked like mews at its further end. The houses on either side of it were narrow with bow-fronted windows and each had delicate fanlights over their pristine front doors. Early Regency, thought Matilda, peering out of her window, and charming. Mr Scott-Thurlow stopped his car, got out and opened her door and invited her to alight, and at the same time a door was opened and an elderly man, very neatly dressed, came down the few steps to meet them.

'Ah, Twigg, Miss ffinch has come to help us with Lucy. Matilda, this is Twigg, who runs my home with his wife. There's a case in the boot, Twigg; I'll come in for a moment but I must leave within minutes. See that Miss ffinch has lunch, will you?'

As he talked he had ushered her into the house and Twigg put down her case and opened a door in the small square hall. It was charming, red-carpeted, its white walls hung with paintings and lighted by wall brackets, and the room which they entered was just as delightful. It overlooked the street, its bow window draped with chintz curtains patterned in soft dim blues and greens and pinks, colours echoed in the magnificent carpet which covered the parquet floor. The furniture was a nice mingling of delicate rosewood cabinets and tables and comfortable sofas and chairs. Matilda, taking one swift look, approved of it; it was exactly to her taste and despite its elegance it exuded an atmosphere of cosiness.

Mr Scott-Thurlow waved her to a chair. 'I do apologise for rushing you like this. As I said we can have a talk this evening; in the meantime Mavis and Twigg will look after you. But first I will take you up to see Lucy.'

They mounted a graceful curving staircase at the back of the hall to the narrow gallery above. There were several doors here but he turned down a narrow passage leading to the back of the house and opened one of the doors at its end. The room was large and light with a big window overlooking quite a sizeable garden. It was charmingly furnished with white-painted furniture and flower-patterned curtains and quilt and Lucy was sitting up in the bed, her small face rendered grotesque by the mumps, flushed and hot but instantly overjoyed at the sight of them. There were two dogs on the end of the bed, one of which was Theobald, and Matilda hardly recognised him, for he was now well fed and very clean, a happy tongue lolling out of his foxy little face. The other dog was a golden Labrador with a gentle face. They got off the bed and Mr Scott-Thurlow caressed them as he advanced to the bed.

'Your Theobald,' he said to Matilda, 'and this is Canada.' He bent to kiss the small girl holding her arms out to him.

'Here is our Lucy. Say hello to Matilda, darling; she has come to keep you company.'

Matilda bent to kiss the child and was held in a throttling embrace. 'I knew you'd come—Uncle James said you would. You're the next best thing to my mummy. Will you live here?'

'Well, until you're fit enough to go to school and by then your mummy will soon be home again.'

Mr Scott-Thurlow put a hand on her arm. 'Mavis will be here presently to show you to your room and answer your questions. Then you will have lunch of course.' He bent to kiss Lucy again, disentangling himself gently from her small arms and went to the door, where he paused, turned round and came back again.

'I haven't thanked you,' he told Matilda and bent his handsome head and kissed her too.

Matilda opened an indignant mouth to utter the scathing words on her tongue and then she thought better of it; Lucy was watching. 'Daddy always kisses Mummy when he has to go away,' she remarked.

Matilda conjured up a bright smile and stooped to pat Theobald. She looked composed when she lifted her head just in time to see Mr Scott-Thurlow disappear through the door, Canada at his heels.

'Why Canada?' she asked.

'She's a Labrador,' Lucy explained kindly. 'Didn't you think of that?' and then, 'You won't stay away for long, will you?'

The door opened then and Mrs Twigg came in, a stout elderly woman with small bright eyes in a round cheerful face. 'Welcome, Miss ffinch, and I hope you'll be happy with us. I'll take you to your room if you're ready to see it now and Twigg has laid a nice little lunch for you in the dining-room. Ever so glad we are that Lucy will have you. I've done me best, miss, but I'm not so young any more. She's a dear little girl and no trouble.'

She exchanged a beaming smile with Lucy and Matilda said, 'I won't be long, darling. Do you have a little nap in the afternoons?'

'Sometimes, but I'll read my book and wait until you come back—may I call you Matilda too?'

'Of course you may.'

Matilda was led away but not very far. Her room was in the corridor too, at the side of the house with a window overlooking a corner of the garden. It was just as pretty a room as Lucy's, furnished in some pale wood she thought might be yew. It had fitted cupboards along one wall and a bathroom, tiled in very pale pink and equipped with everything a girl might need.

'I hope there's all you want, miss,' said Mrs Twigg, 'and just you ask if there is anything at all that we can do for you.'

'It's lovely, Mrs Twigg. Would you like me to come down now for lunch? I can unpack later.'

She followed Mrs Twigg downstairs again and into a fair-sized room opposite the drawing-room where Twigg was waiting.

'A glass of sherry, Miss ffinch? You will take soup?'

She lunched with a good appetite; the food was delicious and Mrs Twigg was a splendid cook. Mr Scott-Thurlow might be a very busy man, she reflected, but when he wasn't being busy he had all the creature comforts he could wish for.

She went back presently and found Lucy hot and restless.

'Another nightie?' she suggested. 'And I'll bathe your face and hands, shall I? Then you'll feel cooler.'

Which she did and then shook up the pillows, gave Lucy a drink and suggested that she should read to her. The child looked ill and very feverish, and since there was a thermometer in a little jar on the dressing-table she took her temperature. It was over a hundred and one and after a little muddled arithmetic she decided that was over forty degrees Celsius. A bit high, but Mr Scott-Thurlow would certainly have been keeping a check on that. She settled down close to the bed and opened *The Lion, the Witch and the Wardrobe* and began to read.

Presently Lucy fell asleep and Matilda sat in the quiet room with no other sound but Theobald's gentle snores. After a while she got up silently and went to her room, leaving the doors open, and unpacked the few things she had brought with her and then went back to sit quietly again; when Lucy woke she would probably be cross and hot and thirsty.

She was all of these things and she wanted her mother. Matilda sponged her small swollen face, mopped her tears, gave her a drink and wrapped her in one of the light wool blankets on the bed before sitting her down on her lap.

'You shall tell me all about Mummy and Daddy, and if you want to cry go ahead, darling, and I won't mind a bit.'

Lucy sniffed mightily. 'You really don't mind? Rhoda says I'm a cry-baby.'

'Pooh to Rhoda. Tell me—is your Mummy pretty?'

Lucy embarked on a description of her mother, pausing for a little weep now and then. She was very hot and Matilda wondered if she should have left her in bed. At least the child was calmer now. She was wondering what was best to be done when there was a knock on the door and Mrs Twigg came in.

'A nice cup of tea,' she said in her soft voice. 'I'll put the tray on this little table so's you can reach it. There's ice-cream for Lucy too. Mr James said as how she could have that.'

'Why doesn't Uncle James come home?' Lucy wanted to know.

'He'll be here in no time, my pretty. Just you let Miss ffinch get her tea while you eat your ice-cream.'

'Her name's Matilda.'

Mrs Twigg looked at Matilda.

'No one ever calls me Miss ffinch...'

'Well, then, Miss Matilda, will that do?'

Lucy nodded a satisfied head and Mrs Twigg trotted off. Matilda longed for a cup of tea; it had been a strange day and she was getting tired. She hadn't phoned her mother yet, her hair was springing loose from its pins and she hadn't even gone round the house to find her way about the place.

Lucy ate her ice-cream and promptly went to sleep, leaving Matilda to clasp her in her arms and watch the teapot, trying to work out a way of reaching it without waking the child up.

The minutes ticked by and all Matilda could think about was how to get a cup of tea; the more she thought about it, the thirstier she became.

Ten minutes passed as slowly as ten weeks, then the door opened and Mr Scott-Thurlow came in. He took in the situation at a glance, and without speaking went to the bed, tidied it, rearranged the pillows, came to Matilda and scooped Lucy off her lap and tucked her into bed. She didn't stir as he took her pulse and felt her head.

'Drink your tea,' he advised Matilda. 'Has it been here long? Would you like a fresh pot?'

'This is quite all right. Do you want some?'

'I had a cup at the hospital.' He sat down in a chair opposite hers. 'How has she been this afternoon?'

'Hot and tearful but she cheered up and ate her ice-cream. She went to sleep all at once before I could get her back into bed.' She added, 'She's feeling wretched, isn't she, poor moppet?'

He leaned forwards and handed her a plate of small sandwiches. She took one and offered them to him. He looked hungry.

He took one and said, 'Now let us go over the routine for you. You will be busy enough for the next few days but by then Lucy will be feeling better and you will have some time to yourself. Mavis will take over from you for an hour in the afternoon—not long, I'm afraid, but you can sit in the garden. Have you phoned your mother?'

She gave him a limpid look. 'No.'

He frowned. 'That was a silly question. Go and do it now as soon as you have had your tea. I'll stay here.'

So she finished her second cup and hurried down-stairs and found Twigg to ask where she could phone. There were, it seemed, phones in almost all the rooms; she went into the drawing-room and found Canada lying before the open french window and bent to pat her, wondering when anyone had the time to take the dog walking. Her mother answered her when she rang but she didn't waste time gossiping. 'I'll write,' she promised. 'I must go back to Lucy now. Everything is fine.'

Lucy was still asleep with she went into the room, and Mr Scott-Thurlow was asleep too, lying back untidily in his chair, his long legs stretched out before him so that she had to step over them to get to her chair.

She sat and pondered as to whether she should wake him or not. He had said that he wanted to talk to her, tell her what her duties were; on the other hand he probably needed his sleep. She studied his face lovingly and was suddenly aware that he was watching her from half-closed eyes.

He began without preamble, 'Your duties are vague, I'm afraid—a surrogate mother is the nearest to them and you are, as far as I can make out, the only one whom Lucy fancies in the role.'

'Surely there must be aunts or cousins or—or what about Miss Symes?'

She shouldn't have said that. He said in a voice as bland as his face, 'Her aunts and cousins are scattered far and wide and I don't quite know why you should mention Rhoda.'

'Why shouldn't I mention her?' she snapped. 'She's going to marry you and I should have thought you would have asked her—she knows Lucy.' She gave him a fiercely defiant look, her insides quaking at the expression on his face. Ferocious was the only word for it.

'I do not think that you need to concern yourself with the whys and wherefores, Matilda. If you would be good enough to listen without interrupting, I will give you some idea of what you may expect from day to day while you are here.'

His voice was coolly civil as he outlined her duties. He was brief too and when he had finished he asked, 'Is there anything else you would like to know?' and when she shook her head, 'Then I suggest that you have a breath of air in the garden. I shall be here for half an hour or so.'

So she found her way out of the house through a small side-door and wandered up and down between the flower-beds, feeling miserable. She had been silly to have dragged Rhoda's name into it in the first place, it was none of her business anyway. She would have to apologise...

She went back presently and found Lucy awake and sitting on his knee, sharing one of her picture books with him, but as she went in he popped the child back into her bed.

'I'll be in my study if you should want me. Twigg will let you know when dinner is ready. Lucy has had rather an exciting day; I dare say she will eat her supper and go to sleep very quickly.'

He went to the door and Matilda followed him. 'I'm sorry I was rude,' she said, 'I can't think why I spoke like that.'

He smiled down at her. 'I have always understood that redheads have a habit of speaking before they think. You are no exception.'

After he had gone she busied herself getting Lucy washed and into a fresh nightie before her supper of soup and more ice-cream, and that done she fetched a book and began to read to the child. It was a favourite of Lucy's and of Matilda's too, *The Secret Garden*, and she stopped frequently to talk about it for they both agreed there could be nothing nicer than having a secret place where one might go, and at Lucy's suggestion Matilda undertook to accompany her when she was well again to see if such a place could be found.

'You're really very nice,' said Lucy and fell asleep, and ten minutes later Mrs Twigg arrived soft-footed. 'Twigg's just about to serve dinner, miss, if you'd like to go down.'

'Have I time to tidy myself, Mrs Twigg?'

'No need, miss, there b'ain't no guests this evening.'

So she went downstairs, rehearsing in her mind the kind of conversation she would have with Mr Scott-Thurlow. The weather was safe enough, and Roseanne's leg, Theobald and his grandparents—there were plenty of innocuous subjects.

'In here.' His voice came from the drawing-room and she went in, surprised to find him in a dinner-jacket. 'You have time for a drink,' he told her and offered her a chair. 'I'm dining out but Twigg will see that you have everything you would like.' He poured her a glass of sherry. 'I dare say you're tired; it has been a busy day for you.' He sounded uninterested.

'No busier than yours, I should think,' said Matilda, determined to be polite. 'I expect you have very little time to yourself.' Her eyes fell upon Theobald and Canada, sitting side by side, their eyes on their master. 'Whenever do you get time to take the dogs for a walk?'

He smiled a little. 'Before breakfast—Twigg takes them during the day and I walk them again before I go to bed.'

She drank her sherry too quickly. 'I expect you want to go out ...'

'As soon as Rhoda arrives. You must stay a moment and meet her.' His voice held amusement and his eyes gleamed with it when she said,

'Oh, yes, that will be delightful.'

Rhoda came a few minutes later and Matilda, twiddling her empty glass in her hand, wished she hadn't tossed off her sherry quite so quickly.

Rhoda looked lovely, but then she always did. Vivid green satin under an enormous velvet cloak and Italian shoes with gleaming buckles. She pecked Mr Scott-Thurlow's cheek and said, 'Darling, you're actually ready. I'm so glad—the Mathersons' dinners are always such fun and one meets all the right people— prospective patients for you ...' She laughed and Matilda watched the look of distaste hidden at once behind that bland mask.

He said, 'Matilda has arrived, you see. Lucy is delighted and so am I to be able to leave the child in such capable hands.'

Rhoda smiled across at Matilda. 'Can you nurse as well as cook?' she wanted to know. 'You really are a paragon.' She didn't hide her scorn.

To which piece of rudeness Matilda could find no answer. It was Mr Scott-Thurlow who spoke. 'Some day some lucky man will make her his wife.' He smiled across the room at Matilda as he said it and she smiled back, dully conscious that she felt suddenly shy, and Rhoda, watching them both, said quite sharply,

'Well, we had better be going, darling. Come back to my place after the Mathersons'—there are so many plans ...'

She nodded at Matilda as she went out of the room, but Mr Scott-Thurlow paused by her chair. 'Breakfast is at eight o'clock,' he told her. 'I hope you sleep well. Goodnight, Matilda.'

She ate her solitary dinner presently under the kindly eye of Twigg. The food was delicious but she hardly noticed what she had on her plate. She was entirely occupied with the unsuitability of Rhoda as Mr Scott-Thurlow's wife. She would ruin him, or try to—turn him into a fashionable surgeon when really what he wanted to do was to use his skill upon anyone who needed it, never mind if they could pay or not. That he was a wealthy man was apparent to her now but she had the feeling that it was a matter of little importance to him. She wondered for the hundredth time why on earth he was going to marry Rhoda.

She thanked Twigg for his attentions and went back upstairs to find that Lucy was soundly sleeping and, since she had nothing better to do, she had a leisurely bath and went to bed herself.

She was up soon after six o'clock, roused by Lucy's small unhappy voice demanding a drink, to have her bed made more comfortable and someone to talk to.

Matilda pottered to and fro making the child comfortable, and since it was still so early suggested that she should go on with *The Secret Garden*.

'I'm thirsty,' declared Lucy, 'I'd like a cup of tea.'

Matilda quite fancied one herself. 'All right, why not? I'll pop down to the kitchen and make us some. I'll have to boil a kettle so don't expect me back for about five minutes.'

The house was quiet as she went downstairs, hoping that the dogs, who probably slept in the kitchen, wouldn't bark when they saw her. She went through the baize door at the back of the hall and crept into the kitchen. It was a delightful place with a well-scrubbed table and rows of polished pans on the walls and an old dresser with rows of plates. There was an Aga too but her eye fastened on an electric kettle.

She filled it, switched it on, peered around for the dogs, who were nowhere to be seen, and went in search of a teapot and cups.

She had made the tea, found milk and sugar and a tray and was on her way to the door when it was opened and the dogs came dashing in followed by Mr Scott-Thurlow in elderly trousers and a cotton sweater.

If he was surprised he didn't show it. His 'good morning' was polite and slightly questioning.

'Lucy woke early, she wants a cup of tea.' Matilda was very conscious of her hair all over the place and her dressing-gown, flung on without due regard to her appearance. She looked at the dogs, grinning at her from either side of their master. 'You've been out,' she said foolishly.

'Our usual morning walk. Is there a cup of tea for me?' When she nodded he picked up the tray and, accompanied by the dogs, they went upstairs.

Lucy was delighted. The dogs got on to the bed and settled down beside her and Mr Scott-Thurlow put the tray on a bedside table and sat on the bed too. 'Slept well?' he wanted to know. 'Stick out your tongue...'

Matilda poured the tea and sat down primly in a chair by the window to drink hers. When she was asked she said that yes, she had slept very well and that no, Lucy hadn't wanted anything during the night.

He finished his tea and got up to go. 'Breakfast at eight o'clock sharp,' he reminded her. He wandered over to the door and stood there looking at her. 'Get dressed first,' he said softly.

She dressed with ferocious speed, muttering crossly to herself, and scraped her glorious hair back into a tight French pleat, under a false impression that it made her look severe, whereas it made her look like a little girl whose hair had been pinned up out of the way ready for her bath.

When she went downstairs she went straight to the kitchen for Lucy's tray only to have it taken from her by a respectful Twigg. 'I will see that Lucy has her breakfast, miss—Maisie, here,' he nodded towards a young girl making toast, 'will come with me and stay with her until you have had your own breakfast. Mr Scott-Thurlow is in the dining-room already.'

So she went to the dining-room to find him there at the table, reading the paper. He got up when she went in, seated her and invited her to help herself to whatever she wanted.

'You don't find this too early?' he asked her politely.

'Not at all. Only shouldn't I be with Lucy?'

'No. I've been to see her again. Her temperature is down, which is a good sign, but I must warn you that as she improves she is likely to be peevish. I rely upon you to cope with that.'

He maintained a steady flow of small talk until they had finished the meal; he was, she conceded, a very good host although she found his reserve chilling. He got up to go presently with a word of apology. 'I seldom get home for lunch,' he told her, 'but I should be back rather earlier than usual this afternoon.

Remember that you should get out for an hour after lunch. Mrs Twigg will sit with Lucy.'

He laid a hand lightly on her shoulder as he went past her chair. Long after he had gone she could feel the imprint of it there too.

That evening, strolling in the garden after her solitary dinner, she reflected that she had enjoyed her day despite the fact that just as they were sitting down to dinner Mr Scott-Thurlow had been called to the hospital, and now, two hours later, there was still no sign of him. Twigg had told her that this was often the case and there was no knowing when he would return, 'So just you enjoy your dinner, Miss Matilda, and take a turn in the garden; it's a splendid evening.'

She had been kept busy during the day with Lucy, who, just as Mr Scott-Thurlow had predicted, was inclined to be peevish, but she had devised games and read until her throat was dry and the child had settled down for a nap after lunch so that she was able to go for a quick walk in the quiet streets near the house while Mrs Twigg sat and knitted in Lucy's room. When she had returned there was just time to freshen up Lucy before her godfather, true to his promise, came home and they had tea together. He had looked tired, but he had set himself to amuse the child and the little meal was a happy one.

When it was quite dark she went indoors, made sure that Lucy was asleep and took herself off to bed. She was pleasantly tired but she didn't go to sleep—she lay awake listening for Mr Scott-Thurlow's return. It was one o'clock in the morning before she heard his quiet tread on the landing and the gentle closing of his door.

The days slipped easily into each other and by the end of a week Lucy was very nearly her old self again. She had the run of the house and she and Matilda spent a good deal of time playing duets on the piano in a small sitting-room at the back of the house. The child was talented and Matilda played with verve and a great many wrong notes and they enjoyed themselves hugely. They saw very little of Mr Scott-Thurlow for now that Lucy was out of her bed she and Matilda breakfasted after he had left the house. He himself had suggested it in a manner which led her to assume that he didn't wish for their company at that meal, and, since he came rarely to lunch at his own house and when he did dine at home his cool courtesy towards her successfully put a stop to any remarks she might make other than mundane ones about the weather, she rapidly reached the conclusion that he disliked her. If that was so, however, why had he asked her to come and look after Lucy?

Even that melancholy thought couldn't stop her loving him.

The days were warm now and she took Lucy out into the garden where they played clock golf, much hindered by the dogs. Nothing more had been said about their visit to Stoke Fleming and Matilda began to hope that he had decided not to send them away. Perhaps he would take a holiday himself and go somewhere with Lucy and Rhoda, for she herself wouldn't be needed for much longer—an opinion not shared by Rhoda, who arrived one afternoon shortly after Matilda had tucked Lucy up for her rest and then had gone downstairs to sit in the garden.

Her greeting was perfunctory. 'How can you bear to sit in the sun?' she asked, and arranged herself carefully in the shade of some artfully planted silver birch trees. 'Where's that child? Isn't she well yet? It's high time she was sent down to Devon; I absolutely refuse to have her tagging around any longer. James has his nose buried in that wretched hospital all day and half the night and I'm sick of making excuses for him. I'll talk to him and get him to send you both away, then perhaps he will be able to lead a more civilised life again. You can stay down there until she's due back at school...'

Matilda's eyes opened wide. 'Oh, that won't be possible; I came to look after Lucy until she was well again, and she is now, so I am free to go home.' She smiled sweetly. 'Why can she not go on holiday with you? I understood that she had been invited to spend the whole of her summer holidays with Mr Scott-Thurlow.'

'Who cares what you understood?' asked Rhoda rudely. 'He pays you so you'll do what he wants.'

'Perhaps he doesn't want me to go to Stoke Fleming...' Matilda's voice was pure syrup.

Rhoda laughed. 'We'll see about that...'

'What will you see about, Rhoda?' asked Mr Scott-Thurlow from the french window.

'Darling, how you startled me. We were discussing plans. Matilda is looking forward to going down to the cottage with Lucy——'

'No, I'm not,' said Matilda. She spoke pleasantly but her green eyes blazed.

Mr Scott-Thurlow lounged over to where she was sitting so that she felt obliged to look up at him looming over her.

'Now that is a pity,' he said gently, 'for I have arranged for you to go down to Devon in two days' time.'

CHAPTER EIGHT

MR SCOTT-THURLOW had an 'I told you so' look on his handsome features. 'I did mention that you would be going to Stoke Fleming as soon as Lucy was well enough and since you raised no objection I went ahead with my plans.'

Rhoda gave a brittle laugh. 'There, did I not say so? How lucky you are getting a holiday for free, Matilda. Darling, I'll cancel my engagements—where shall we go? Will you get tickets? Do be sure that the hotel is a good one—will it be too hot in the Bahamas?'

He had been staring at Matilda and she had been unable to look away for his gaze held hers but now he turned to Rhoda. 'I'm committed to a seminar in Leiden and a couple of lectures in Oslo and I must be back as soon as possible—I have a backlog of urgent cases...'

A speech Matilda heard with satisfaction and Rhoda with ill-concealed temper.

'What am I supposed to do?' she wanted to know. 'Don't think I'm trailing round Europe while you make dreary speeches about bones. The Burches asked me to go to Bangkok; I shall go with them.'

'It sounds delightful; there is no reason why you should get bored while I lecture. Besides, there would be little time to spend together; these sessions carry their quota of dinners and drinks parties and I'm ashamed to say that we all talk shop.'

'I suppose you're going back to that beastly hospital or rooms until midnight or longer. We're supposed to be at dinner with the Burches, or had you forgotten?'

'No, I phoned my excuses half an hour ago. They're expecting you and said they would get another man.'

Matilda, watching Rhoda, saw how her ill temper had made her quite ugly; it was a pity that Mr Scott-Thurlow hadn't seemed to notice that for he was smiling at Rhoda quite charmingly.

'I'm going,' said Rhoda coldly.

He went with her into the house and presently returned to where Matilda was still sitting.

'Have you nothing to say?' he asked. 'I feel sure that you are bottling up a number of searing speeches calculated to put me in my place.'

'Well, I am, but what would be the use?'

'None at all, so swallow your dudgeon and listen to me... You will be kind enough to get your things together tomorrow and Lucy's too, telephone your family by all means—I have already told your mother. I will be here by eight o'clock on the day after tomorrow, so be ready to leave then. We should get to the cottage by lunchtime. There is a housekeeper, my mother's cook, pensioned off—her name is Emma Truscott, and she will have everything ready for you both. Please get Lucy out of doors as much as possible but don't let her get tired. But I don't need to tell you this—you're a sensible young woman. In just over two weeks she must return to school, when your duties will end.'

'Why should I do this?' demanded Matilda. 'You come here without a by your leave——'

'It is my house,' he reminded her blandly.

'You know very well what I mean, Mr Scott-Thurlow; I feel as though I'm being—being trampled underfoot.' She glared at him and looked quite enchanting. 'Do this, do that, go here, go there! I don't know why I put up with it.'

'Yes, you do, Matilda.' He watched the colour flood into her face. 'But when you address me so severely as Mr Scott-Thurlow I realise what a despot I am.'

He sounded so meek that she wanted to laugh and did.

'That's better. Shall we have tea out here? Go and get Lucy and I'll tell Twigg.'

Lucy was enchanted with the idea of going down to Devon. She plied her godfather with questions while they had their tea until he said, 'I must get back to my rooms—I have several patients to see.' He got up and stopped to receive Lucy's hug and kiss. 'Remember to be ready to leave promptly,' he reminded Matilda. He hesitated, staring down at her, smiling wryly, but he didn't say anything, only nodded briefly as he went.

It was Twigg who told her that evening that Mr Scott-Thurlow had gone to Birmingham to operate at one of the hospitals there. 'Some tricky case, I'll be bound, Miss Matilda; he gets called all over the place, so he does.'

They were up early on the day of their departure and went down to breakfast soon after seven o'clock to find Mr Scott-Thurlow already at the table. His 'good morning' was genial and followed by the observation that he was delighted to see them up so promptly.

'Will you stay at the cottage with us?' asked Lucy.

'No, I shall have to come back here this evening; I'm going to Leiden tomorrow.'

'You will come down and see us though?' Lucy persisted.

'Well, we'll have to see about that. Shall we take Canada and Theobald with us?'

Matilda and Lucy chorused, 'Of course,' and two pairs of eyes gave him an indignant look. 'They don't see much of you anyway,' declared Matilda.

His smile was mocking. 'Sometimes I suspect that you would wish to change my life for me, Matilda.'

She choked over her coffee. 'Certainly not,'

She spoke with such vehemence that he laughed. 'You're not much good at telling fibs,' he told her.

They set off in good time with Lucy on the back seat, Theobald on her lap and Canada sitting very erect beside her. Matilda settled into her seat beside Mr Scott-Thurlow and cast about for harmless topics of conversation. She tried the weather, the charm of the country, the pleasure of driving early in the day and so on, then since she had received nothing but grunts and monosyllables in reply, lapsed into silence.

Presently he said, 'You have no need to make small talk with me, Matilda, I am very content to drive with you silent beside me.'

At which remark she drew a long, smouldering breath. 'If you will stop for a moment I will change places with Lucy...'

He answered her seriously, although she suspected that he was laughing to himself. 'No, no that won't be necessary. Have I offended you? I'm sorry; I haven't had much practice with pretty speeches.'

'Well, it's time you had,' said Matilda wrathfully. 'You'll have to change your ways when you get married.'

'I suspect that they will be changed for me.'

She frowned; it had seemed to her that Rhoda would be quite content with a husband who was absorbed in his work and left her free to live the social life she seemed to love. She uttered her thoughts out loud.

'Has she gone to Bangkok?' The words were out before she could stop them, but before she could do anything about it he answered her in an ordinary voice with no surprise in it.

'Yesterday. The Burches were delighted that she could go with them; I imagine that she will enjoy herself enormously.'

Matilda muttered a reply, very red in the face, and he, glancing quickly at her, smiled slowly and then said over his shoulder, 'I thought we'd stop presently, Lucy—would you like that?'

They were north of Salisbury by now, still on the A303, and it was after they had passed Wincanton that he said, 'Your mother suggested that we might stop for coffee,' and turned off on to a side-road. 'We can't stay long but you will have the time to collect anything you may want.'

'Thank you. May Lucy go into the sea?'

'If the day is warm and she stays only a short time. Do you wish to swim?'

'Yes.'

Then they didn't speak again until he drew up outside her home.

The entire ffinch family came out to meet them; Matilda wondered if Mr Scott-Thurlow was comparing the warmth and noise of their reception with the cool and perfect manners of Rhoda. It was impossible to tell from his expression and his own manners were too good to give her a clue. Lucy, instantly made much of, was borne away to the kitchen by Esme to be refreshed with cake and lemonade while the rest of the party strolled after them. The kitchen door was open and the sunlight streamed in to the comfortably shabby room, smelling of freshly ground coffee and newly baked cakes. Matilda saw Mr Scott-Thurlow's splendid nose twitch appreciatively.

'You're in a hurry,' said her mother, 'so I thought it better if we had coffee here—Tilly, you'll want to run upstairs and collect some clothes, I suspect. Hilary put everything out on the bed, ready to pack. If you'll just pick out what you're going to want, my dear.'

'I'll go now, while you're pouring the coffee. Thanks, Hilary...'

She flew upstairs and found the elderly zipper bag they all borrowed in turn in the bedroom and a couple of cotton dresses neatly pressed and folded. Her swimsuit was there too and some old sandals, just right for the beach. She packed the bag, added a thick sweater in case it turned chilly and went back to the kitchen, to find everyone there, some sitting at the table, the younger ones milling around, in and out of the garden.

Mindful of Mr Scott-Thurlow's wishes, she gobbled her cake, swallowed down her coffee and pronounced herself ready to leave, but another ten minutes was wasted while she made her protracted goodbyes and the dogs were rounded up and they were all stowed into the car once more.

'What a pity you can't go and see your grand-parents,' said Matilda at the end of her polite speech of thanks. 'You practically pass their door...'

'No time. I'll call on my way back.' They were again on the A303 and he sent the Rolls forwards at the steady maximum speed allowed. They joined the A30 presently and then turned off on to the motorway south of Exeter. Here he could travel faster and the big car shot effortlessly ahead, eating up the miles, and so on towards Plymouth and to the road over Haldon and then the long straight stretch to Buckfastleigh and Totnes and all too soon—from her point of view—they were on the road to Kingsbridge.

'This is the long way round,' said Mr Scott-Thurlow, 'but it is by far the prettiest road.' At Kingsbridge he took the road to Torcross and then raced along Slapton Sands with the beach on one side of them and a charming lake on the other, and at its end he took the car smartly up the steep wooded road which led to the village.

Stoke Fleming rambled on either side of the road; small white and pink painted cottages with thatched roofs and gardens bright with flowers, and splendid views of the beach and sea below. He turned the car down a narrow lane and in through an open gateway and stopped before the open door of a traditionally pink-washed cottage, its thatched roof pierced by small lattice windows and surrounded by a fair-sized lawn and a wealth of flower-beds. He leaned over to the back seat and opened the door for Lucy and the dogs and got out himself to go round to Matilda's side.

'Why, it's pure heaven!' she told him. 'What a pity that you can't stay here too—you need a holiday.' She waved an arm. 'All this space and the view and this darling little house...'

She became aware that he was looking at her and smiling. As usual, she reflected crossly, she was allowing her tongue to chatter on. She looked away from him and said stiffly, 'This seems a charming place; Lucy will love it.'

The child and the dogs had rushed into the house; she could hear Lucy's voice, squeaky with excitement, and a moment later she came running out again, this time with a small round woman, grey-haired and rosy-cheeked.

She went straight to Mr Scott-Thurlow, who hugged her, kissed her soundly and told her in a voice Matilda had never heard before—it was so content—that she was prettier than ever. 'And this is Matilda,' he told her, 'come to keep this imp of mischief out of trouble and keep you company.'

Matilda smiled at the nice kind face as she shook hands; they were going to like each other. She said happily, 'I'm sure we're going to be very happy here.'

'No doubt of it, me love. And as pretty a maid as I seen for many years. Now just you come in and eat your dinners and you, Mr James, must have a nice lay-down before you go back. More's the pity that you have to go.'

She bustled them indoors, through a small hall and into a large, low-ceilinged room with a table set under the far window; the floor was polished and spread with thick rugs and the chairs were comfortable and well cushioned. A matronly cat sat in one of them, washing herself, taking no notice of the dogs pottering to and fro.

'You'll be wanting to tidy yourselves,' said Emma Truscott. 'Up the stairs and the first door on the right—don't be long, I'll be dishing up.' As she trotted off into the kitchen Matilda heard her telling Mr James to fetch the cases, do, and take them up to the bedrooms.

When they went downstairs again there was an old-fashioned soup tureen on the table and Mr Scott-Thurlow was ladling its contents into deep plates. Matilda sat Lucy at the table. 'Can I do anything to help, Miss Truscott?'

'Call me Emma, me love, and sit yourself down. Watercress soup I made myself and as nice a chicken as ever I saw to follow.' She cast Matilda an approving look. 'Enjoy good food, do you? You're a nice healthy shape—I don't hold with all this fancy eating; I like a woman to look like one. Don't you agree with me, Mr James?'

Matilda bent a red face over her plate. Mr Scott-Thurlow gave a serious reply but she had no doubt that he was amused.

The chicken was brought in, carved with the expertise expected of the carver, and eaten with the appropriate trimmings and followed by raspberries and clotted cream, while Emma enlarged on the various small events in the village. All too soon the meal was over and Mr Scott-Thurlow was preparing to leave.

'You'll not go, Mr James, until you've sat yourself down for ten minutes, quiet like. Dear knows what your insides will be like if you get straight into that car of yours and go dashing off.'

It surprised Matilda that he did as he was told and went to sit outside in a garden chair with nothing but the sea in front of him. Lucy climbed on to his lap and sat quietly while Matilda helped clear the table. At the end of ten minutes, he got to his feet, hugged the child and said in a voice which meant what it said that he was leaving.

'Well, if you must, you must,' grumbled Emma, 'but just you take care how you drive.'

He said 'yes' meekly, hugged her fondly, kissed Lucy and nodded to Matilda. However, halfway to the gate he paused and came back to her, put his hands on her shoulders and kissed her. It was a tender, lingering kiss and she thrilled to it, aware that if he had dropped his guard the kiss would have been quite different. She turned her back on good sense and kissed him back, knowing that she would regret it bitterly.

He said nothing at all but turned on his heel, got into his car, and with a wave of his hand, drove himself away.

She turned round to see Emma eyeing her thoughtfully. She said breathlessly, 'I expect he thought I was Rhoda...'

A silly remark which received a tart answer. 'You know and I know that he thought no such thing, love. Now you go and unpack your things and take Lucy down to the beach. There's a path down the cliff to the shore, through the wicket gate at the bottom of the garden.'

The sand was firm and clean, and they strolled along on the edge of the sea, their sandals in their hands, revelling in the warm air and the sound of the water splashing their feet. 'I wish Uncle James was here too,' said Lucy. 'I can't see why he can't have a holiday...?'

'He has to go to Holland, darling—he's a busy man.'

'Do you suppose he'll come and see us while we're here?'

'I don't think so.' Matilda sounded sad; if he had any time at all he would surely spend it with Rhoda.

'Well, I do,' said Lucy, 'he likes me and he likes you too—he kissed you goodbye.'

'Well, that was because he kissed us all, didn't he?'

'He took a lot longer over you,' said Lucy.

They went to bed early, bidden to do so by Emma in her soft West Country voice, so it made sense that they should be up early too, to spend a long day, shopping for Emma, doing a few chores around the house and then going down to the beach, this time with a bucket and spade for Lucy and wearing cheap straw hats to protect them from the sun. All the same Matilda had a sprinkling of freckles across her nose by the evening. She sat at her dressing-table that evening, rubbing them with a cream to remove them and which did no such thing. Not that she minded much; there was no one to see them, and by no one of course she meant Mr Scott-Thurlow. She jumped into bed and inspected her room with pleasure. The cottage was charmingly furnished with the right kind of furniture, pretty chintz curtains and soft rugs. It had been skilfully modernised but it still contrived to look cosy despite the porcelain ornaments scattered around the silver tableware and fine linen. It was, reflected Matilda, a home—a retreat. She wondered how often Mr Scott-Thurlow came to stay in it and if Rhoda had ever been with him. It was a pity that she couldn't ask Emma...

But she had no need; over breakfast the next morning Emma volunteered the information that Mr James, when he came to stay for a few days or a weekend, came alone. 'That Miss Symes he's supposed to wed came to visit one afternoon—she can't a-bear this end of the country; likes the bright lights or foreign parts. Dear knows how they'll sort that out when they marry, if ever they do.'

Matilda murmured vaguely, glad that Lucy had left the table to take the crumbs for the seagulls, and Emma went on chattily, 'You've seen quite a bit of Mr James, I dare say, what with the little dog and his granny and now little Lucy.' She cast a shrewd eye at Matilda. 'He's a good man, is Mr James, as well as being a gentleman born, and you don't often get the two together.' She obviously expected an answer.

'Yes, he's very kind...'

''Andsome too, and then all that money... There's been plenty of young women willing to have him and his money.'

Matilda reflected that she was willing to have him without a single penny piece; she loved him regardless of anything else, but love wasn't enough. She said in a small wooden voice, 'Well, he's found someone he wants to marry...'

She was piling marmalade on to a piece of toast and didn't see Emma's look. 'That he has, me love, and the sooner the better, he's been too long without someone to love him and be loved.' She was suddenly brisk. 'Now, if you'll go, the pair of you, to the butcher's and fetch some of his sausages we'll have toad-in-the-hole for our dinner and there's raspberries to be picked in the garden. You'll be going to the beach presently?'

Matilda got up with a sense of relief. Emma was a darling but her eyes were sharp and she seemed to know a great deal about James—well, of course she would, having been cook to his parents and then joining his grandparents' household until he had installed her as housekeeper in this cottage. He wasn't mentioned again that day and indeed no one mentioned his name during the next few days, which slid with pleasurable slowness into a week, during which the pair of them acquired a glorious tan and Lucy, under Matilda's patient guidance, learned to swim. They also developed healthy appetites. 'I shall get fat,' declared Matilda, helping herself to more clotted cream. They went for gentle strolls in the evenings once the supper had been cleared away and the dishes washed, leaving Emma to sit with her old-fashioned specs perched on the end of her nose, reading the paper, and on Sunday they all went to the village church before going back to Emma's splendid Sunday dinner. Quite perfect, thought Matilda, or almost quite—if James were there it would be . . .

The lovely weather showed no sign of abating. Matilda got up early while Lucy still slept and got into one of her rather elderly cotton dresses, tied back her hair and went downstairs to give a hand with the weekly wash. There was a washing-machine of course and she had engaged to keep it filled and emptied while Emma got the breakfast. With all the doors and windows open, and the morning already pleasantly warm even at seven o'clock in the morning, she went happily about the task. Emma had put the first load in earlier; Matilda piled the clothes basket, loaded the machine again and went off to where the clothes-line hung out of sight at the bottom of the garden. It was pleasant hanging up sheets and towels and pillow-cases with no sound but the waves below, the seagulls on the look-out for breakfast and a car or two on the road, going down the hill to Slapton Sands, intent on finding a vacant parking space before everyone else got there. She finished ramming home the last peg, picked up the basket and went back to the cottage; Emma would have breakfast ready by now.

She put the basket in the scullery ready for the next load and went through the open kitchen door. Mr Scott-Thurlow was leaning against the wall, talking to Emma, frying bacon on the Aga. He was wearing an open-necked shirt and drill trousers and had the air of someone who had been on holiday for some time.

Matilda fetched up short, frowning fiercely because she felt the bright colour flood into her face, but she couldn't stop the happy sparkle in her eyes.

He studied her face for a moment. 'Good morning, Matilda.' His eyes left her face and travelled over her person, giving her time to regret the elderly dress. 'You look well—Emma's cooking, no doubt . . .'

'If you mean I've got fat——' she began wrathfully.

'No, no, nothing of the sort. You appear to me to be—er—exactly the right shape. And Lucy?'

'Is splendid—she's put on weight too and she looks marvellous.'

'That makes two of you.'

She didn't answer that. 'Have you just got here?' she asked politely.

'I got here about three o'clock this morning.'

'Three o'clock . . . But you ought to be in bed, you must be tired out.'

'Not a bit of it. I've given myself two days off so I hope that you—and Lucy—will bear with my company.'

She couldn't prevent the wide smile and when he smiled slowly too she actually took a step towards him, wanting to be near him, tell him how happy she was to see him. It was providential that Emma spoke.

'Bacon's done to a turn and there's the tatties fried up how you like 'em. Sit down, do, and eat your breakfasts.'

Matilda dragged her eyes away from Mr Scott-Thurlow's face. 'I'll fetch Lucy.' She flew out of the room and up the little staircase and found the child hanging out of the window. 'I heard some dogs barking, they sounded just like Canada and Theobald, but it's not of course. I was looking to see if there's anyone on the beach...'

'Come down and eat your breakfast, love,' said Matilda, and laughed out loud when she saw the child's delight and surprise when the dogs came to meet them at the kitchen door.

Lucy burst into the room. 'Uncle James, you're here, it was Theobald barking and Canada!' She flung herself at him, talking excitedly, and it took a few minutes before they were all sitting at the table intent on breakfast.

Mr Scott-Thurlow ate an enormous meal, but then he was a very large man and probably he hadn't had his supper or stopped on the way down.

'Are you here for weeks and weeks?' asked Lucy.

'Two days, sweetheart, so tell me what you want to do most and we'll do it.'

He looked across the table at Matilda as he spoke, and because there was something in his face which she found disquieting she said quickly, 'It's going to be a lovely day.'

A silly remark, but he agreed with her, still staring at her until the slow lovely colour crept into her cheeks. He smiled then and looked away and Lucy broke the silence.

'I can swim, Uncle James—can we go down on to the beach and I'll show you? I do six strokes if Matilda is beside me.'

'I can think of nothing nicer. Emma, have I got some swimming gear somewhere?'

'In the airing cupboard, ready and waiting.' She beamed at him and offered more toast.

'Could we have a picnic lunch in the garden? All of us—sandwiches and so on. Would it upset your plans if we had our dinner in the evening? I'd hate to miss any of this wonderful sun...'

'Anything you say, Mr James,' said Emma. 'It's a treat to have someone in the house. I am going to miss you when you've all gone.'

'I promise you we shall come back again, Emma.'

Matilda, watching Emma's face, knew exactly what she was thinking—if Rhoda were to come she would prefer to be on her own, thank you.

Breakfast over, James astonished Matilda by doing the washing-up while she and Emma cleared the table and set the place to rights again and then went to make the beds.

'Don't be long about it,' he called after them. 'Lucy, feed the dogs, will you? Everything is ready on the garden table.'

So presently, their chores done and leaving Emma to have what she called a nice sit-down, they went down the path to the beach. The tide was on the turn and it was already warm. Matilda sat down against a convenient rock, rammed her wide straw hat over her bright hair and delved into the large straw bag she had brought with her. She had prudently got into her swimsuit and donned her dress on top of it, feeling shy of James, but Lucy's childish bikini was there, and so were three cans of lemonade, a bag of doughnuts, some Dettol cream and some Band-Aids. There was a paperback there too, but she didn't think she would have a chance to read. She hoped she wouldn't.

Her hopes were realised; Mr Scott-Thurlow was transformed from a rather unapproachable consultant surgeon to a godfather willing to do anything within reason. They built a tremendous sand-castle with a channel running down to the water and a moat around it and then they sat eating their doughnuts while the tide came in and washed it all away again.

'Time for a swim,' said Mr Scott-Thurlow and stripped off his shirt and trousers, caught up Lucy in a giggling bundle and waded into the water, leaving Matilda to peel off her dress and follow them.

Lucy had to demonstrate her swimming prowess and, that done, sat happily enough on the beach with the water washing around her feet while Matilda and Mr Scott-Thurlow swam strongly out to sea and back again, and once back they lay, the three of them, with the gentle waves washing over them, soaking up the sun. The tide was coming in, so they got up reluctantly and went to sit out of reach of the water, and presently at Lucy's insistence they built another sand-castle. Matilda, obediently filling buckets of sand and handing it over to the builders, thought what a splendid father he would make and lost herself in a daydream peopled by a horde of little Scott-Thurlows, herself and James, so that she was only aroused by repeated shouts for more sand.

They had their picnic in the garden with Emma and then lay about doing nothing until it was time for tea. After tea, in the cool of the late afternoon, they went walking. Down the hill to Slapton Sands, still packed with day visitors, to walk along the sands, bare-footed, splashing along on the very edge of the sea. When they got back to the cottage they showered and changed and sat down to one of Emma's delicious meals. Garlic mushrooms, roast chicken with all the trimmings, a pile of roast potatoes and asparagus, creamed spinach and baby corn, and one of her fruit pies with a crust which melted in the mouth and loaded down with clotted cream.

They sat over the meal until Matilda gathered up Lucy, already half asleep, and bore her off to her bed. When she came down Emma had taken the coffee into the sitting-room and they sat over that too. Presently Mr Scott-Thurlow suggested that a stroll along the sand would be pleasant on such a splendid evening, so Matilda fetched a cardigan and slung it around her shoulders and accompanied him down to the beach once more.

'You really ought to go to bed early,' she told him. 'You shouldn't burn the candle at both ends.'

'Afraid I might let the knife slip? I have never met a girl who was so anxious to order my life for me, Matilda.'

His mocking voice hurt her and wakened her quick temper. 'Don't talk nonsense—I don't imagine there is anyone on this earth who can do that, and if there is it's Rhoda.'

'You are mistaken. Nothing and no one, save one person, will have the power to change my life.'

She had her mouth open to ask who the someone was and then snapped it shut; it wasn't her business, but did it mean that he wasn't going to marry Rhoda? She said in her best social manner, 'What a delightful evening it is; we're having a marvellous summer.'

He answered her with a hint of a laugh in his voice. 'Indeed, yes—the most marvellous summer of my life.'

Which wasn't quite the answer she had expected; she worked away at her small talk and he politely followed her lead and in a little while they went back to the cottage and said goodnight.

The next day followed the pattern of the previous one only there was no stroll in the evening, for after dinner, eaten a little earlier than usual, Mr Scott-Thurlow prepared to leave.

'Must you go?' asked Lucy tearfully.

'Yes, but I'm taking my two lovely days here back with me, aren't I? And who knows, I may come again before you go back to school. In any case I'll come and fetch you back to London and take you back to Miss Tremble's.'

He swung her up in his great arms and kissed her soundly and then hugged Emma. 'Dear Emma, thank you...' He kissed her pink cheek with affection. Matilda, standing a little apart, wondered if they should shake hands, or would he give her a friendly nod as he went?

He did neither; he put his hands on her shoulders and kissed her too, another gentle, lingering kiss which sent her pulses racing and took her breath, but not quite all of it for she kissed him back, flinging good sense to the winds again, never mind the future, never mind Rhoda, this moment was hers.

Mr Scott-Thurlow straightened his imposing height and then stood looking at her. He said nothing at all but bent once more and kissed her again, this time swift and hard.

They stood at the cottage door waving him goodbye. 'He kissed you twice,' said Lucy. 'I think Uncle James likes you very much, Matilda.'

'Bedtime, love!' said Emma. 'You uncle likes us all and what a lovely time you've had these last two days. Eaten us out of house and home, he has—tomorrow you and Matilda will have to go shopping for me. You can get the bus into Dartmouth.'

She bustled the child upstairs, which gave Matilda a few minutes in which to pull her disordered thoughts together and regret very bitterly that she had returned Mr Scott-Thurlow's kiss. It had been heaven, of course, but now she went scarlet with shame at allowing him to find out her feelings for him, for she had certainly made no secret of them. She frowned; his kisses had been rather more than friendly...

There was a letter from Esme in the morning, full of family news and bits of gossip about the village. One of the maids at the manor-house was going steady with the milkman's son, Lady Fox had a new and quite awful hat, Sir Benjamin had fluffed his lines reading the lesson on Sunday and Nelson the cat had caught a rat at the bottom of the garden. 'And I must tell you,' wrote Esme in her impetuous scrawl, 'who do you suppose came to see Mother the other day? That Rhoda woman who's going to marry our nice Mr Scott-Thurlow; she'd been to see Roseanne, who's almost well—and called in on her way back to

London. Said what a lovely time she and he were
having—parties and so on—I didn't believe half of
it. Said what a pity it was that Roseanne wouldn't be
able to be one of the bridesmaids since she and Mr
Scott-Thurlow are getting married very shortly. I hate
her.'

So do I, thought Matilda bitterly. His kisses hadn't
meant anything, just a last fling before he married.
She hoped that she would never see him again. She
looked at the letter once more. Esme wrote that Rhoda
had actually said that she would send Matilda an invitation to the wedding because she had been so kind
and capable.

'Pah!' said Matilda with such force that Emma and
Lucy both looked at her with astonishment.

The days, empty of Mr Scott-Thurlow's presence,
went slowly by. They did the same things, went for
the same walks, played the same games and spent a
good deal of time messing about on the beach and in
the water. Matilda made no mention of him and was
outwardly cheerful as usual but Lucy observed a dozen
times a day that she wanted him back.

'You're a very nice person,' she explained to
Matilda, 'and so is Emma, but it's not quite the same.'
Tears weren't far off. 'And it's almost time for me to
go back to Miss Tremble's.'

'It's also almost time for your mummy and daddy
to come home, love, only another week or two...'

There was no word from Mr Scott-Thurlow, not
until their very last day when he phoned to say that
they could expect him for lunch on the following day
and they were to be ready to leave in the early afternoon. So Matilda packed their things and took Lucy
down to the beach for their last morning bathe and,

while they were gone, Emma, listening to Mr Scott-Thurlow's voice on the phone once again, chuckled comfortably at what he had to say.

The next day—the last, thought Matilda gloomily, alternately thrilled at the thought of seeing him again and still smarting from Esme's letter—they went down to the beach just once more. She had laid their clothes ready for travelling and left enough room to stuff their cotton dresses in at the last minute; she hadn't bothered about make-up either, or her hair, which she had tied back with a handy piece of string from the kitchen.

They were building a sand-castle to end all sand-castles when they heard the dogs—Canada's gruff unhurried bark and Theobald's excited yap. Coming towards them were three people: Mr Scott-Thurlow and a man and a woman.

Lucy flung down her spade. 'Mummy! Daddy!' she bawled, and tore to meet them.

CHAPTER NINE

MATILDA stood still and watched Mr Scott-Thurlow and the dogs coming towards her; he wasn't hurrying, which gave her time to get over the rapture of seeing him and stoke up her indignation at his behaviour, so that when he reached her she returned his cheerful greeting in a witheringly chilly, calm voice which sent his eyebrows up.

'Surprised you? Matt and Jean got back yesterday, several weeks earlier than they had expected. They'll stay here and keep Lucy with them—Matt has already spoken to Miss Tremble—and they'll take her with them when they go to Berkshire. You're ready to leave? Good. I'll take you back with me and drop you off at Abner Magna—I have to be back in town this evening.'

He didn't wait for her reply, which was just as well. 'Come and meet Jean and Matt . . .' He stood towering over her, smiling, looking, she reflected, a bit smug. 'I like the string,' he told her.

She gave him a haughty look. 'We weren't expecting you—we came down here for a last hour or two and naturally we couldn't wear the clothes we shall travel in.'

'Lucy won't be travelling. Anyway, I like that chemise thing you're wearing.'

She got rather pink; the white cotton dress she was wearing was sleeveless and with a scooped-out low neckline—a well-worn garment she had kept for messing around with Lucy, but before she could answer him he was introducing her to Lucy's parents and presently the whole party made their way back to the cottage. Once there, he made no attempt to engage her in conversation but wandered off into the garden, leaving her to gossip gently with Jean while Lucy sat between them bubbling over with happiness.

'We are so grateful to you,' said Jean. 'James says you're marvellous with children, animals and sudden mishaps—you've certainly been a fairy godmother to Lucy. He didn't tell us how pretty you are. No, not pretty—beautiful, and I love your hair.'

'I'm not very tidy, I'm afraid. I'd better go and change; I expect Mr Scott-Thurlow will want to leave directly after lunch and I mustn't keep him waiting. He's giving me a lift home.'

Jean gave her a nice smile. She was tempted to tell this delightful creature in her simple clothes just what James had said about her, but that would never do; besides, they had a long drive before them, ample time for them to talk. 'I'll unpack Lucy's clothes, shall I? I've brought one or two things with me.' She dropped a kiss on her daughter's head. 'Would you like to see them now, darling?'

So the three of them went upstairs and Matilda had a shower and got into the flower-patterned two-piece, stuck her stockinged feet into neat shoes, did her face and brushed her hair into its severe French pleat. Surveying her reflection, she thought that she hadn't looked like that for more than two weeks.

Mr Scott-Thurlow had meant what he said when he had told her that they would leave immediately after lunch. He stowed her case in the boot, whistled to the dogs, bade everyone a brisk goodbye and then waited with no sign of impatience while Matilda said her own farewells. Prolonged hugs from Lucy and promises to meet again, reiterated thanks from her mother and father and a rather tearful one from Emma, who pressed a dozen brown eggs and a pot of cream on her with the fervent hope that Matilda would come and see her again. A rare pity, she thought as she watched the beautiful Matilda get into the car, that her Mr James hadn't chosen to marry her instead of the haughty creature who, on her one visit, had ignored her completely.

They all waved at the departing car and Emma said, 'Ah, well, it's a nice long drive.'

Jean smilingly agreed; she had only met Rhoda once and she hadn't liked her either. She had no doubt that she and Emma were thinking the same thing.

It was Lucy who put their thoughts into words. 'It would be nice if Matilda and Uncle James got married,' she said.

If they had been in the car they would have had their doubts. Matilda, sustaining a polite flow of small talk in a frosty voice and encouraged to do so by an amused James, was as unapproachable as a bed of stinging nettles. Presently he said, 'We have a long drive ahead of us—could you stop being so polite with your chit-chat and be you?'

She wouldn't look at him. 'I'm sure I don't know what you mean.'

'No? Ah, well—all in good time. Let us continue with our small talk. Did you know that Roseanne is getting married in September? The wedding is to be a very grand affair.'

It was on the tip of her tongue to ask him if his own wedding would be grand too; she couldn't imagine it to be otherwise with Rhoda as the bride. She checked the question just in time and was rewarded by his, 'A wedding should be a family affair with only close friends, do you not agree?'

'Well, yes. Everyone else only comes out of curiosity.'

The car ate up the miles in a well-bred fashion and he kept the talk undemanding, lapsing into long silences which strangely enough left her perfectly at ease with him. They also gave her a chance to think, and her thoughts were sad. This was probably the last time she would be with him; their paths were unlikely to meet in the future, and a good thing too for it was hard to maintain her chilly politeness.

They were nearing Montacute on the A303 and not far from Abner Magna now when he turned off into a side-road.

'You've gone off the road,' said Matilda unnecessarily.

'We are having tea at Grandmother's.' He glanced at his watch. 'It's barely four o'clock—just right. We're expected.'

'But Mother is expecting——'

'Around half-past five or six o'clock.'

Mackrell Cantelo basked in the afternoon sun and the village was quiet as he swept through it and turned in at the stone pillars. As they stopped before the house Slocombe came through the door to meet them.

'A pleasure to see you, Mr James and Miss ffinch. Your grandparents are in the conservatory—I'll bring tea there in a few minutes. Perhaps you would like to freshen up, miss?'

Matilda smoothed her hair, applied more lipstick and tidied her already tidy person and then went back into the hall. Was she supposed to find her way to the conservatory on her own? she wondered. Apparently not; Mr Scott-Thurlow was sitting on the stairs waiting for her. She might have known that he would be; he was so thoughtful of other people. She hoped that Rhoda appreciated that.

His grandparents were sitting in peacock chairs overshadowed by palms, ferns and clinging greenery. The doors to the terrace were open but even then it was warm. The dogs made a beeline for the lawn outside and she envied them as she greeted her hostess and, obedient to Mrs Scott-Thurlow's request, sat down beside her.

'It is delightful to see you again, my dear,' said the old lady. 'Now you must tell me about your stay at Stoke Fleming. Such a dear little cottage, is it not?'

The talk was general and pleasant over tea and presently the old lady said, 'Why don't you two young people have ten minutes in the garden and take a little stroll before you go? My roses are glorious and you really must see them.'

Matilda was surprised when Mr Scott-Thurlow got up. 'A splendid idea—come along, Matilda.'

Her inclination was to refuse, but with the old lady's kindly eyes fixed upon her that would have been impossible. Crossing the lawn with him, the dogs wreathing around them, she said with some asperity, 'I thought you were in a hurry?'

'Oh, I am, but I have found that there is always time for something one wishes to do.'

'Oh, yes, the roses.' They had reached the end of the large garden where the rose-beds made a splash of lovely colours, the beds separated by closely cut turf paths.

He came to a halt, staring down at her with a faint frown. 'What is the matter, Matilda? When I was at the cottage I thought ... Well, never mind that now.' He put his hands on her shoulders. 'You have always been frank and outspoken,' he smiled a little, 'too outspoken sometimes, but you are hiding something and I wonder why?'

'I don't know what you're talking about ...'

She drew back from him and he let her go at once. 'In that case I'll not say what I wanted to say to you; I should have told you at the cottage.'

She said fiercely, 'Well, I'm glad you didn't for I don't want to know.'

He stared down at her thoughtfully, his face calm and unworried. 'No? If ever you should change your mind, Matilda, you know where to find me.' He smiled suddenly. 'And having admired the roses we had better be on our way.'

They made their farewells and the two old people came to the door with them and watched them drive away, the dogs once more on the back seat, Matilda sitting rather erect beside James.

'A dear girl,' remarked his grandmother. 'She will manage him very well.'

Abner Magna looked peaceful in the late afternoon sunshine and the rectory garden, untidy and a little neglected though it was, was full of colour. Their welcome was warm for everyone was at home and anxious to greet them, but Mr Scott-Thurlow, in a few well-polished sentences, made his excuses, bade them all goodbye and got back into his car, the reluctant dogs climbing in once more. He had said all the right things; Matilda had been of the greatest help and Lucy had grown very fond of her, in fact he was indeed very grateful and hoped that he hadn't hindered her in getting some more congenial job. He had wished her goodbye with a bland smile and eyes as hard as blue steel.

'A pity he couldn't stay for supper,' said her mother, 'but I dare say he wants to get back to town. Did Esme tell you in her letter that Rhoda Symes came here, Tilly? Full of her wedding arrangements, said to be sure and tell you because you'd be interested. I don't like her.'

'Now, now, my dear,' said the rector mildly, 'we must try and like everyone.'

For once his wife disagreed with him. 'You can't like someone you don't like,' she told him with female logic.

The busy, happy life at the rectory was soothing to Matilda. Just for a moment she had felt sudden happiness at the sight of the envelope addressed to her in James's illegible handwriting, which someone had put on her dressing-table. She had opened it with a shaky hand and found a cheque inside and a businesslike slip of paper, typed no doubt by his secretary and signed with his initials. She would have liked to have torn it into little shreds and sent it back to him, but for once good sense had the ascendancy over her red hair. The cheque was for a tidy sum; it meant football boots for the boys, a new hat for her mother, a longed-for book for her father and clothes for Esme, Hilary and herself. She had put it in her purse, sniffed away a great desire to cry and gone downstairs to her supper.

She had been home for a few days when her mother came back from the village. 'I met Lady Fox, Tilly—

she had heard that you were back and Roseanne wants you to go and see her.' She glanced at her daughter's beautiful and sad face. 'I hope I did the right thing in saying you would go. She's coming home in a few days now but Bernard has had to go away and she's longing for company. Esme's too young and Hilary doesn't want to talk about anyone else's wedding except her own.'

Matilda rubbed butter into flour, intent on making an apple tart. 'I'll go tomorrow if Father will let me borrow the car.'

It was a quiet morning with the faint haziness of late summer in the air. She drove slowly while she thought. Once the boys were back at school and Esme back at her school, she would get a job, somewhere where there was no chance of meeting James, somewhere where no one knew him so that when he married Rhoda she wouldn't know about it, and then in no time he would become a memory, getting more and more vague until she couldn't remember what he looked like, and that would leave her free to marry some man who wouldn't rock her heart and send her pulses racing. Even as she thought it she knew that the very idea was nonsense; she would never forget him...

Roseanne was sitting outside on the hospital veranda and professed herself delighted to see Matilda, proudly demonstrating the fact that, excepting for a gutter crutch, she was well again.

'Of course, by the time we marry I shall be able to walk without the wretched thing. I must tell you about the wedding...' Something she did at great length; indeed she hadn't finished when she was interrupted—one of the sisters came through the open door on to the veranda and with her came Mr Scott-Thurlow.

He saw Matilda at once but his face remained impassive. Nothing could have been more polite than his 'good morning', uttered in a pleasant voice before he turned his attention to Roseanne.

'I'll go,' said Matilda, praying feverishly that he would say that she might stay. Only he didn't, merely waited until she bade Roseanne goodbye and then nodded and smiled at her, at his most urbane. The impetuous side of her nature longed to throw something at him but the loving side wept silently at his bland indifference.

The hospital was away from the main road, and Matilda started to drive back to Abner Magna along the network of country roads which would eventually take her home. They were quiet, used mainly by farm vehicles and people who had lost their way, and the villages were few and some miles from each other. The country here was open with splendid views and low, rolling hills. It was halfway up one of these that the engine coughed, laboured on for a few yards, coughed again and stopped.

'Now what?' enquired Matilda of the surrounding quiet and got out and looked under the bonnet—a useless exercise for she had only the vaguest idea as to what was underneath it. It looked the same as usual. She got back into the car and pressed the self-starter; nothing happened, and it was then that she saw that there was no petrol. 'Halfway up a hill, too,' she exclaimed. 'Now what?'

'What' materialised in the shape of a car coming with effortless ease up the hill. It came to a smooth halt a few yards ahead of her and Mr Scott-Thurlow got out. He walked unhurriedly to her car, stuck his head through the window and observed mildly, 'Not a very good place to stop, but no doubt you had your reasons.'

She bristled. 'As though anyone with any sense would stop halfway up a hill...'

He glanced at the dashboard. 'Out of petrol?' He shook his head in a particularly infuriating manner. 'And I thought you were such a sensible girl.'

'I *am* a sensible girl,' she snapped and tossed her fiery head at him. 'Anyone can run out of petrol.'

'Of course,' he said soothingly. 'One only needs to forget to fill up.'

Her eyes gleamed greenly. 'Don't let me keep you—someone will come along presently—or perhaps you would be so kind as to stop at Dunn's garage—it's a mile or so along this road, just before you get to Littlecote-sub-Magna...'

'I will be even kinder—I will put some petrol in your tank for you.' His smile mocked her. 'I carry a spare can or two.'

She might have known that he would; he was a man who was prepared for all eventualities. She watched him go back to his car, fetch the petrol, empty its contents into her tank and return the can to his own boot. He did it without haste and very tidily and then walked back again and opened her door. 'Move over,' he told her.

'Why?'

He glanced at the few yards between the cars. 'I don't want the Rolls to get bashed. So move over, dear girl; much as I would like to waste my time in your company I have to get back to town.'

She moved over. 'You had no need to stop,' she muttered crossly.

'That is one of the silliest remarks I have ever heard; a pity I haven't the time to tell you why.'

He drove her car up to the crest of the hill and stopped. 'Off you go,' he told her as he got out. 'And for heaven's sake drive carefully.'

A remark calculated to send her shooting along the narrow road as fast as she could. All the same, he overtook her at the bottom of the hill and soared away out of sight without even glancing at her as he passed.

She was still seething when she got home and the sight of Lady Fox sitting outside the drawing-room window hardly improved her temper. Her mother was there too and the coffee-tray and both ladies turned to look at her as she crossed the grass.

Lady Fox was all graciousness. 'Matilda—you have just returned from visiting Roseanne? Does she not look well? Such a splendid job Mr Scott-Thurlow has done on her poor leg.' She sighed loudly. 'Though I shudder to think of his bill. Still, one must have the best, must one not?' She took a good look at Matilda. 'I must say you are rather pale; surely you should have more colour after your lovely holiday in Devon? I heard all about it from Rhoda.'

Matilda accepted a cup of coffee from her mother. 'But she wasn't there.'

Lady Fox looked arch. 'Well, no—she dislikes the cottage, I believe, but Mr Scott-Thurlow spent a couple of days there, did he not? And naturally he would have told her all about it.' She added reprovingly, 'They are engaged, after all.'

'I wonder what will happen when they marry?' mused Matilda out loud. 'Will he spend his holidays at Stoke Fleming and Rhoda carry on with her round of parties?'

Lady Fox's formidable bosom swelled alarmingly. 'Really, Matilda, I don't think that remark is in the best of taste.' She looked away from Matilda's green stare. 'What do you intend to do next?'

'I've no idea, Lady Fox.' She finished her coffee. 'You'll excuse me?' She smiled at her mother. 'I'll get those beans blanched ready for the freezer.'

The two ladies watched her go. 'Such a sensible girl,' said Lady Fox. 'It must be a great worry to you that she is not yet married.'

Mrs ffinch smiled. 'Why should it worry me? Matilda could have married several times over but she is content to wait until she meets the right man.'

'Supposing she doesn't?' asked Lady Fox acidly.

'Oh, but she will, I have no doubt about that.' Mrs ffinch lifted the coffee-pot. 'Will you have another cup?'

Mrs ffinch might have had no doubts about her daughter, but Matilda was a mass of conflicting emotions. She longed to see James again but what good would that do? For when they did meet, she snapped at him and he—he laughed at her even when his face was placid. She must amuse him a good deal and she had been a fool to kiss him. He shouldn't have kissed her in the first place though . . .

She did her best to settle down into the bosom of her family, undertaking rather more chores than she needed to in and around the parish, helping in the house, cooking and gardening. None of these were enough to stop her thinking. She had been at home for just over a week when she told her mother that she had seen a job in the *Western Gazette* and intended to apply for it. 'Someone wants help with an old lady who has gone a bit dotty, I gather. In the Western Highlands . . .'

Her mother, beating batter, paused for a second and then went on calmly, 'It sounds a long way away, darling—and an old lady, senile at that—she would be very trying.' She saw the obstinate set of Matilda's gentle mouth and went on quickly. 'But I dare say a change would be pleasant. They say the scenery is magnificent.'

Matilda thought sadly she didn't care a button about the scenery; it was a long way from James. 'I think I'll write anyway,' she announced and drifted away to find pen and paper, sit down at the little desk in the sitting-room and then fall into a daydream where James came in through the door . . .

Esme came through the door instead. 'I say,' she said excitedly, 'have you seen this?' She waved the *Daily Telegraph* at Matilda.

'How could I have seen it?' Matilda, her daydream interrupted, spoke testily. 'You've got the paper.'

'Well, I'll read it to you. It says, "The marriage arranged between Miss Rhoda Symes and Mr James Scott-Thurlow will not now take place——"'

The paper was whipped out of her hand and Matilda read it for herself, and just to make sure she read it for a second time. He had wanted to tell her something at the cottage and she hadn't let him—he had told her that she would know where to find him if she were to change her mind and yet when he had stopped to give her petrol he hadn't said a word; indeed, he had been at his most tiresome . . .

'What are you going to do?' asked Esme.

'Do, what should I do? It's no concern of mine.'

Esme gave her a thoughtful look. 'You've been in love with James for a long time, haven't you? The least you can do is tell him.'

Matilda looked at her with horror. 'Tell him? I'd sooner die.'

Which dramatic statement was ignored by her sister. 'Rubbish—you do love him, don't you, Tilly?'

'Yes.' Matilda got up so quickly that paper and envelopes flew in all directions. She darted through the door and into her father's study.

'Father, may I borrow the car? Just to get to Sherborne—I want to catch the London train.'

Her father studied her face, usually so serene, and saw that she was labouring under some strong emotion. 'Certainly you may, Matilda. How long will you be gone? I might need it in the meantime . . .'

'Oh, I hadn't thought of that. I don't know, I'm going to see James—Mr Scott-Thurlow—if—that is, I might come back later today—it depends.'

The Reverend Mr ffinch pushed his sermon to one side. 'Hilary will be back from Salisbury this afternoon; ask the station-master to tell her to pick the car up from the station yard. She can drive herself back here.' He glanced at the clock on the mantelpiece. 'You had better hurry, my dear.'

She dropped a kiss on to his thatch of grey hair and tore through the house and upstairs to her room, where she began rooting around in her wardrobe. It had become important that she look her best.

A glance at her watch told her that if she was to catch the train fussing around deciding what to wear wasn't to be considered. She got into the flowered two-piece; he had seen it often enough, but who cared?

She would have liked to have spent some time on her face and hair, but as it was they both received perfunctory attention. She crammed odds and ends into her handbag; at least she had some money...

Her explanations to her mother were garbled and vague, leaving that lady to sort them out at her leisure. She kissed her parent swiftly and ran out to the shed where the car was kept. Esme was there. 'You're wearing that again,' she said, 'but of course if James loves you he won't care if you're wrapped in a sack.'

'I don't know,' said Matilda wildly. 'Sometimes I thought... and then I was sure that he didn't...'

She got into the car and Esme leaned through the open window. 'Well, you'll soon know...' She glanced over her shoulder and luckily Matilda, bent over the ignition key, didn't see her face, wreathed in a wide grin. The Rolls was nosing its way through the open gate and came to a halt. 'Back carefully,' she told Matilda.

The car started up in a middle-aged fashion and Matilda began to back it out of the shed; there was plenty of room to turn at the side of the house. She gave a perfunctory glance in the mirror, gasped with fright and braked within a few feet of theRolls, which was effectively blocking her path.

Mr Scott-Thurlow had got out and so had the dogs. Esme, regretful that she was about to miss an interesting situation, whistled to them and took herself off, round to the back of the house.

Matilda didn't see her go and if Mr Scott-Thurlow did he gave no sign.

He walked without haste from his car to hers, opened the door and waited while she got out.

'Going somewhere?' he wanted to know.

She was trembling with the excitement of seeing him and the shock of very nearly backing into the Rolls. She said in a shaky little voice, 'I almost backed into your car. I could have damaged it.'

He had taken her hands in his. 'Rolls-Royce motor cars don't damage easily. Were you coming to see me?'

When she nodded he said, 'I thought that you might. You are a very obstinate girl, my darling—that is because of your lovely red hair, of course, but I do hope that, when we are married, you will listen meekly when I have something to say to you. Of course until this moment there has been very little opportunity.'

'Don't you love her?'

'No. And I never did. How delightfully direct you are, dear heart.' He smiled down at her. 'I love you, and deep in your heart you know that. I loved you the moment I saw you in church. I wanted to marry you there and then, but of course that wouldn't have been very practical, and besides I had to end my engagement to Rhoda. All the while I wasn't sure if you loved me.'

'How could you possibly know? I never said a word.'

He smiled slowly. '"There's language in her eye, her cheek, her lip..."'

'Shakespeare, *Troilus and Cressida*,' said Matilda, momentarily diverted. 'Then why didn't you——?'

He bent and kissed her very gently. 'Dear heart, when did you ever give me any encouragement?'

'You don't need encouragement,' she told him flatly. 'You know just what you're doing with your life; you're successful and nothing seems to disturb you—you're so calm.'

'My dear life, I can see that you know nothing about me at all. You will have years in which to discover just what kind of man I am.' He plucked her close and wrapped her in his great arms. 'There is one thing you must learn immediately. I do not care to waste time.' He kissed her then, and there was nothing gentle about it this time.

'Oh, my goodness,' whispered Matilda when she had her breath again. 'What——?'

'Marry me, Matilda. You can ask me anything you want once we are married, but there is one question. Do you love me?'

'Yes, oh, dear James, you have no idea how much.'

'I shall enjoy finding out, my darling heart. We had better tell your family, had we not? But first . . .'

He pulled her close to kiss her soundly and the ffinch family, watching unashamedly from a variety of windows, sighed their satisfaction. Her father went down to the cellar to fetch up a bottle of champagne he had been saving for some special occasion; her mother, arranging glasses on a tray, reflected with guilty satisfaction that Lady Fox was going to be put out and, as for Esme, she was dreaming up her bridesmaid's dress.

Not that any of these things mattered to the two people standing so close together in the drive; they had found their heaven and they were content.

Following the success of WITH THIS RING, Harlequin cordially invites you to enjoy the romance of the wedding season with

BARBARA BRETTON
RITA CLAY ESTRADA
SANDRA JAMES
DEBBIE MACOMBER

A collection of romantic stories that celebrate the joy, excitement, and mishaps of planning that special day by these four award-winning Harlequin authors.

Available in April at your favorite Harlequin retail outlets.

Janet Dailey
Americana

Janet Dailey's perennially popular Americana series continues with more exciting states!

Don't miss this romantic tour of America through fifty favorite Harlequin Presents novels, each one set in a different state, and researched by Janet and her husband, Bill.

A journey of a lifetime in one cherished collection.

April titles   **#29 NEW HAMPSHIRE**
Heart of Stone

#30 NEW JERSEY
One of the Boys

Harlequin Regency Romance™

WHO SAYS ROMANCE IS A THING OF THE PAST?

We do! At Harlequin Regency Romance, we offer you romance the way it was always meant to be.

What could be more romantic than to follow the adventures of a duchess or duke through the glittering assembly rooms of Regency England? Or to eavesdrop on their witty conversations or romantic interludes? The music, the costumes, the ballrooms and the dance will sweep you away to a time when pleasure was a priority and privilege a prerequisite.

If you are longing for the good old days when falling in love still meant something very special, then come to Harlequin Regency Romance—romance with a touch of class.   RRG

HARLEQUIN Temptation

Rebels & Rogues

Jackson: Honesty was his policy...
and the price he demanded of the woman
he loved.

THE LAST HONEST MAN
by Leandra Logan
Temptation #393, May 1992

All men are not created equal. Some are
rough around the edges. Tough-minded but
tenderhearted. Incredibly sexy. The tempting
fulfillment of every woman's fantasy.

When it's time to fight for what they believe in,
to win that special woman, our Rebels and Rogues
are heroes at heart. Twelve Rebels and Rogues,
one each month in 1992, only from
Harlequin Temptation!
